P9-DNE-607

Coming to Terms

ALSO BY ANNA MURDOCH

In Her Own Image

Family Business

COMING TO TERMS

A NOVEL

ANNA MURDOCH

HarperCollins*Publishers*

FIRST U.S. EDITION

Designed by Helene Berinsky

Library of Congress Cataloging-in-Publication Data
Murdoch, Anna.
Coming to terms / Anna Murdoch. — 1st U.S. ed.
p. cm.
ISBN 0-06-018303-9
I. Title.
PR9619.3.M73C66 1991
823—dc20 90-55967

91 92 93 94 95 CC/HC 10 9 8 7 6 5 4 3 2 1

In memory of my father
Jakob Torv

Coming to Terms

Prologue

I still miss Uncle Percy.

I got to thinking about him the other day when the cap broke off my tooth and I couldn't get to the dentist. Uncle Percy could fix anything.

I thought if I could just write down the way he was I could bring him back to me, smell that funny old smell of his: part tobacco, part wood shavings, part old man's sweat. But then I realized I didn't know the whole story, so I had to ask the family to fill in the bits.

Joelene told me most of it—and George, of course. Even Pete contributed. And Frank O'Malley, the state trooper—well, he helped me with Ernie and Don's side of things. That was before he gave me a speeding ticket on the Taconic and clammed up. And of course I had my journal.

But there were lots of bits that no one really knew, so I admit some of them I made up and others I had to intuit. There's more than one way of knowing things. The funny thing is that now I can't tell which bits are more true than others.

One

My cousin Joelene Mathieson came to look after Uncle Percy in the middle of October the year before last. Her visit changed all our lives.

It had been an exceptionally cold early fall, and Uncle Percy had nearly been taken by the Good Lord to his Bosom in Heaven through the convenience of pneumonia. But Uncle Percy made it clear that he was not ready to go and struggled out of his hospital bed and stood with a blanket over his shoulders and his purple feet planted on the polished floor and bellowed to get him out of there! And so we did, and he came home.

There was a family conference, most of it held over telephones, about what to do about Uncle Percy. He had always lived on his own and refused to go into a home. He was seventy-seven years old, infirm, irascible, and poor. He owned his own house, but that was that. He had never married, so had no children of his own to take over the burden of guilt and debt which would normally have been their lot. There was only a far-flung family of cousins and nieces–greats or grands and once-removeds–spread across the country from the Catskills to the Sierra Nevada. Most of them were young with mortgages and toddlers to take care of; none of them had time for Uncle Percy.

It seemed there was no one who loved Uncle Percy enough to put up with him. Uncle Percy was difficult to get on with. Uncle Percy never bathed. Uncle Percy cussed. You could almost see the telephone lines reverberating as his future was discussed.

"If only there was someone who needed *him,*" said Moira, my mother, and then she had her brainstorm. "Joelene," she said. "We could ask Cousin Joelene if she is free."

"She won't come," said Cousin Bea in Amarillo. Cousin Bea was the widow of one of Uncle Percy's brothers. In this family the term "cousin" is generic. It makes life much simpler, except for outsiders.

"She was a nurse's aide once. I can ask."

My dad thought it sounded like a good idea. He thought this arrangement would bring about two good deeds through dealing with one misfortune: it would bring some comfort and nursing to Uncle Percy, who could not now be left alone, and it would give Joelene a home and a way of escaping from her "problems" without anything untoward having to be said.

So Moira rang Joelene in California and Joelene rang Cousin Bea in Amarillo and Bea said my dad said it was a good idea. And Joelene said yes and set off to drive across country from Santa Monica to Poughkeepsie because she could not afford the plane fare and none of the family thought to offer to pay. Besides, it was well known that Joelene, like her father before her, was afraid of heights, so taking a plane was quite out of the question.

My older sister, Gerry, was on duty in the old redwood house when Joelene telephoned to say she was somewhere west of the Tappan Zee Bridge and would be there within the hour.

"OK if I leave, Uncle Percy?" said Gerry, slipping into her leather jacket after she hung up. "Joelene will be here soon and I'm already running late." It was five in the afternoon and Gerry, who was eighteen then, worked part-time as a waitress at Chuck's Tastee Diner off the Taconic Parkway. She had on her candy-striped uniform and lace apron under her jacket. "I've left a note for Joelene in the kitchen, telling her what pills you have to take and when, OK?"

Uncle Percy's small, alert face stared at her over the top of his bedding. Gerry gave a perfunctory pat to his pillow and rushed out the door.

"I'll leave a light on," she shouted. " 'Bye, now."

Uncle Percy listened to the cough and stutter of her car before the engine kicked in and she drove away. A deep sigh left him. It was the first time he had been left alone for weeks. He swung his legs over the edge of the bed and took a tentative step. Not too good. He groped for a walker standing against the wall and made his way to the bathroom. The bathroom was freezing cold. He had to sit down to pee like a woman, but the relief was so intense that for once he didn't cuss. "O Lord," he said, "be merciful to me, a sinner." Eventually he felt strong enough to stand up and went into the kitchen.

Gerry had left the radio on, and the sound of rock music blasted at Uncle Percy. He pulled the plug out and it stopped. He reached up and took a bottle of tea-colored liquid from a shelf. He had fermented it himself and licked his lips with anticipation. Uncle Percy sat at the kitchen table, cleared himself some space, and poured himself a drink. He coughed. He would have loved a cigarette, but he had given them up in the hospital.

He picked up Gerry's note for Joelene while he drank. He couldn't read most of it. He didn't have his eyeglasses on. Some words written large he could read; TWICE A DAY, and DR. BEAMER'S HOME NUMBER, and DO NOT LET HIM NEAR A HARDWARE STORE. Damn buggers, he thought. He took a draft of liquor and waited for the usual jolt, but nothing happened. He sniffed the bottle. It had been filled with coffee. Moira! he thought. That damn woman had been into everything.

A car crunched to a stop at the front door. Joelene.

Uncle Percy pulled his head into his shoulders like a tortoise. A cunning look came over his face. He heard her call.

"Uncle Percy, it's me, Joelene! Anybody home?" He heard the doors open through the house and then he started to cough. He tried to keep it quiet but Joelene heard him, and the kitchen was flooded with light as she opened the door and found the switch.

"Why, Uncle Percy. You were tricking me after I've driven clear across the country to get here."

Joelene stood like a small bright candle in Uncle Percy's dull kitchen. She wore white slacks and a white top and her short red-gold hair stood up like a flame above her lively face. "I would have been here sooner, but I had trouble with the car. A fuel leak. Last week it was the gasket on the windshield. I've been whistling 'Dixie' in tune with the noise ever since I left California. And no one warned me about the bridge. It's so high!" Uncle Percy's attempt at suppressing his cough had turned into a choke. Joelene opened her pocketbook and took out a flask. It was one of those hip flasks you see advertised in Sharper Image catalogs and others like them, leather and silver and shaped in a curve. Joelene put the flask to Uncle Percy's mouth. Smooth fiery brandy slipped down his throat and deep pink patches appeared immediately on his cheeks.

"Why, if it isn't Joelene," he said, his voice croaking from disuse. "I've jist been hangin' on till you could come." Uncle Percy doesn't say "just," he says "jist"; he doesn't say "get," he says "git."

"I'll bet," she said.

"How are you?" he asked as she slipped her hands under his armpits and helped him to his feet.

"I'm fine, but I've got to get you to bed. This room is as cold as a church at a funeral. Isn't the furnace working?"

But Uncle Percy had fallen back into his silent mode. He was tired. He let her propel him along to his room. She was wearing some white chiffon scarf that tickled his ear.

"I can get into bed myself," he said.

"I'm glad to hear it," Joelene said and stood with her arms folded while he struggled into bed.

He closed his eyes and said, before she closed the door, "And don't you go putting up my furnace. I'm not rich like you Californians, wasting everything, throwing things away."

"Yes, Uncle Percy," said Joelene.

In the hallway Joelene found the thermostat, hesitated for a moment, and then flicked it up to 80 degrees and went out to her car. She wrenched open the door and shook the sleeping form inside.

"Come on, George, honey," she said. "We've arrived."

George honey groaned and writhed and snuggled deeper but Joelene pulled the covers off him.

"Up. Out."

"Christ. It's freezing here," he said, as he tumbled out of the car.

"It's even colder inside. Here, take this. This." She piled sweaters, bags, books on his arms. A white paper bag of gummy bears was thrust into his fist. He towered over her, his long lank hair hanging over his face. She pulled the cords of a Walkman out of his ears. "W-e-l-c-o-m-e," she spelled, "to the great Northeast. Welcome to the house I was born in."

Joelene grabbed two duffel bags from the trunk and lugged them up the steps onto the porch. The house had been built at the turn of the century in a pseudo-Federal style. Two white pillars held up the roof of the porch, and the front door was surmounted by an elliptical fanlight and flanked by narrow sidelights. It all looked very gracious in the dark, the light bulb above having burned out years ago and never been replaced. Joelene pushed the door open to the hall. It was wide and gloomy, lit with a single naked bulb; the wooden floors were stained dark and the walls were dingy with grime. A big old hallstand with a mirror dominated one wall, and on its various hooks and projections hung hats and coats, peaked hats of canvas, and straw gardening hats with frayed crowns and brims which threw lattice-shaped shadows on the wall. Joelene brushed against a matted pea jacket and an old black coat, green with mildew, and checked her reflection in the spotted mirror as she put down one of her bags.

"This can be your room, George," she said, throwing

open a door, "and this can be mine." She went into the next room and hefted her bag onto the lumpy, high bed and turned down the coverlet. There were no sheets. She sat on the edge of the bed and gave the mattress a bounce, but it didn't give at all. She smiled at George in the doorway. "This used to be the best guest room." She poked a finger through the coarse lace that fell from the top of the four-poster and sneezed. She couldn't tell if it was from cold or the dust.

"Can we eat?" George said, yawning. "Where's the old man sleep?"

"Across the hall," Joelene said, getting up. "And don't speak of him like that."

"Like what?" he asked innocently as she brushed past him.

"You know. Go wash your hands. You'll find a bathroom at the end of the hall. I'll rustle up something to eat."

"Well, he *is* old," George said as he went back into his own room.

"Who's there?" shouted Uncle Percy, hearing a strange male voice in the house.

"It's all right," said Joelene, opening the door into his room. "It's only George. Oh, my God!" Uncle Percy sat up in bed with a rifle in his hands. It was his old Winchester, and it was pointing right at Joelene's head.

"Who's George?" Uncle Percy's quivering hands tried to steady the rifle against his shoulder.

"My son. George. Uncle Percy, put that thing down before you hurt someone. Come in, George, and shake hands with your great-uncle."

Uncle Percy lowered the rifle as George came into the room. He had to stoop to avoid hitting the light. He put out his hand.

"Hi."

"Hmmmph." Uncle Percy's eyes lit on George's earring twinkling under the light. " 'Nother damn mouth to feed," he said and closed his eyes.

"Come on," said Joelene, taking the rifle from him gingerly and placing it on the floor. "We're all tired. We'll talk in the morning. Can I get you anything?" But Uncle Percy refused to talk. His mouth had zipped shut and he turned his head away. Joelene waited a few moments and then said, "All right, then, Uncle Percy. See you in the morning," and shut the door quietly.

"What kind of name is Percy anyway?" said George later, sitting in the kitchen with her and eating a fried beef patty between two squares of Wonder bread. "Short for Percival?" He mimicked what he thought was an English accent.

"Pericles," said Joelene, dipping a knife into a jar of mayonnaise and opening her sandwich to add more.

"Worse yet," said George, through a mouthful of food. He was always hungry. "Who's he?"

"You know. Pericles. It was on *Jeopardy!* last week. He was Greek and he had an odd-shaped head. When Uncle Percy was born his head was the shape of a sweet potato, all knobs and elongated. But of course it went down after the trauma of birth was over." Joelene began to peel a tangerine she had found in her pocket. "The family says my grandmother nearly stopped having babies after that. His head nearly killed her." She popped a segment in her mouth and offered one to her son. "But she went on and had Norman and Arthur, one after the other."

"Otherwise I wouldn't be here. Neither of us would. You stopped after me." George looked at her through his long hair, and for a moment she saw the little boy he had once been. She took the dishes to the sink.

"One was enough. My, I used to think I would love to have ten. Children all over the place, and me—a dazzling example of motherhood: calm, organized, understanding"—she threw a tea towel around her shoulders—"and glamorous."

Joelene twirled around and caught her son lighting a joint. All her pretense left her.

"Give me that, George. I won't have it in the house." She took the cigarette from his fingers, broke it, and threw it in the sink. "Why do you do this stuff?"

"Joelene, Joelene," George said. He leaned back on the kitchen chair, threatening to tip it over, and swung one sandal from his stockinged toe.

"And don't 'Joelene' me. I don't like your smoking it. Don didn't like it either."

"I don't listen to anything Don says."

"You don't listen to anything anyone says." She bit back more criticism. "Look, I don't want to have an argument." George stood up and stretched. "Don tried to help you. That's why he gave you a job in the car showroom. But you blew it."

"Sure. And why did you leave, Mother?" She heard the capitalized letter.

"I am mortally afraid of earthquakes."

"Not California, Mom. Don and the showroom."

"You know very well that things didn't work out between Don and me."

"You're afraid of him."

"I am not."

"He hit you."

"He did not. I fell."

Her son's eyes, brown like her own, looked right back into hers. He tossed his hair back from his forehead, hitched up his jeans, and blew her a kiss. "Good night, then, dazzling mother," he said as he went out the door.

Joelene blew out a long breath, made herself another cup of instant coffee, and picked up the note from Gerry.

Dear Cousin Joelene, it began. *Welcome to Poughkeepsie.* Joelene smiled and rubbed the goose bumps on her arms. She would need some warm clothes. *Uncle P's pills are in the bathroom. He takes them* TWICE A DAY. *Change his heart disc each morning. Do not let him in the ark. DO NOT LET HIM NEAR A HARDWARE STORE. DR. BEAMER'S NUMBER IS* (illegible). *Mom will call on you tomorrow. Good Luck.*

Joelene checked Uncle Percy on her way to bed. He seemed to be asleep, though his breathing was labored. She would raise the head of his bed in the morning. The room was icy cold. She went out and closed the door and looked at the thermostat in the hall. It had been switched off. A fine thread was knotted around the metal arrow on the gauge. Joelene followed the thread with her finger. It disappeared under Uncle Percy's door. She gave the thread a tweak and it yanked out of her hand. She smiled and left it where it was.

In her room Joelene found some sheets in a drawer, made up the bed, and unpacked her few belongings; two pairs of jeans, a skirt, a beaded fluffy sweater, a blouse or two. She hung up her clothes in the squeaky-doored wardrobe, with its jangling, rusty dry-cleaners' hangers. She noticed there was a strong, earthy smell in the room. It was not unpleasant, and she wondered what it was. She placed a large dog-eared Webster's dictionary on the night table along with an old copy of *House and Garden* with a picture of a pink California house with purple bougainvillea on the cover. Then she unpacked her survival kit, an ax with a red-painted wooden handle, a yellow plastic hard hat, and a large bottle of water, and placed them in a straight line between her and the door.

Bending down, she noticed the earth smell was even stronger and decided it came from under the bed.

Joelene got on her hands and knees and pulled out a large cardboard carton of potatoes. Uncle Percy must have stored them there at the end of the season. They were pink and firm and still nestled in the earth they had been pulled from.

Joelene sat back on her heels, breathed in deeply, and for the first time since she had arrived was flooded with memories. She remembered early summer evenings when she would be sent out by her mother to rob the potato plants. She remembered tickling along the roots with her bare hands until she found the first early fingerlings and then patting the earth back into place. Her mother, also called Joelene, and her father, Norman, and sometimes Uncle Percy, too, would be sitting on the back porch watching her through the screens. Joelene had felt proud, loved, attended, when she showed them the little potatoes.

She remembered it vividly now as she undressed quickly, kicking at fluff balls with her feet, and jumped into the freezing bed under the sagging cream-colored lace. She ignored the scratchings of what she thought must be a mouse. Tomorrow. All would be put to rights tomorrow. She began to make a list in her head. From her son's room next door she heard faint strains of music, and she could smell, under the earth smell of the potatoes, another smell, drifting and sweet. Damn him! thought Joelene, and added another item to her list of things to do. Oh, yes, one other thing was bothering her. What on earth did Gerry mean by an ark? Perhaps, in her haste to go she had left off a letter. P-a-r-k. That must be it. She was not to let Uncle Percy in the park.

Two

Uncle Percy's redwood house stands on a street that has seen better days in a town near Poughkeepsie in the Hudson River Valley. There is no road sign to direct you there—it fell down years ago and has yet to be replaced. There is no postal delivery, because the house lies outside the town limits. The nearest country store is two and an eighth miles east, under the Thruway and at a junction of five crossroads that acts as a square.

The country store is a red frame building with white woodwork, and a gray cat sits in the window on top of all the newspapers and magazines: not the *New York Times* but the *Post,* and not *Vogue* or *Elle* but *Gun and Rod, Automobile,* and *L.L. Bean* catalogs. There is a fire station and the siren goes off at noon and six o'clock, so everyone can check their watches or go to lunch or have a Budweiser at the Inn before they go home. It's called the Inn but no one stays there; it's just a bar. There is a gas station, too, but it is never open. All the new developments—the high-tech offices in landscaped acres and the shopping malls surrounded by parking lots—all those took place on commuter routes zapping right off the Thruway.

Uncle Percy's town, our town, got cut off somehow, bypassed, and people left. Even the church lost its pastor, and everyone has to drive to Poughkeepsie now to attend a service. That is, those who are still believers. There is sometimes a little activity in deer season when the woods behind the house crawl with men in bright orange vests. No one likes the hunters. Once a hunter came up to the house in back and told Uncle Percy he was lost. But Uncle Percy got out his own rifle and pointed it at him and said, "Git off my land!" and the fellow scampered. He must have thought Uncle Percy would really use the gun. He can look fierce sometimes.

After breakfast Joelene said she had to go shopping. There was very little food in the house. She had made a bowl of rolled oats for Uncle Percy but he had refused it after the first mouthful. "Cain't you cook, woman?" he said and spat the oats out on the floor. Now Joelene would be the first to admit she can't cook, but Uncle Percy hurt her feelings and she mopped up the mess with tears in her eyes. Later, she had taken in a bowl of hot water to give him a bedbath, but he wouldn't let her near him. He hooked his fingers through the wire bedstead and refused to let go, just lay there hollering at the top of his voice, "What d'you want to do, give me pew-monia?" Joelene was too soft to say that, well, frankly, Uncle Percy smelled, so she gave up—for the time being. Now she sat making a list in the kitchen.

George loped in from visiting Uncle Percy. The commotion had woken him up. "His head don't look too bad to me," he said. Joelene wasn't listening. A small glass jar with a screw-top lid stood empty on the table.

"I found thirty dollars and change," she said. "Housekeeping money."

George began looking for some food. He prowled around the kitchen with his hair falling in his face.

Joelene looked up. "You're in charge, George, while I'm gone." She sucked her pencil. "I need a chair to get your uncle into the shower."

"You can't leave me here," said George, hitching an extra T-shirt over his head. "We're in the middle of nowhere."

"We're in Poughkeepsie—nearly."

"And he might die!"

"He won't die—not till I get back." Joelene got up and looked in a cabinet and then sat down and added something to her list. "He'll just lie quiet as a lamb until I return."

George stumbled to the refrigerator. There was nothing to eat. He opened the freezer, took out a packet of freezer-burned waffles, dropped one in the toaster. He made himself instant coffee with hot water from the faucet. While he was busy, Joelene leaned over and went through the pockets of his jacket hanging on the back of a chair. She found the packet she was looking for, slipped it into her pocket, and sat back innocently. George had noticed nothing. He slumped into the chair with his coffee mug.

"Mom, what are we doin' here? He's got people here who could help. Why you have to come here from California—"

"I told you, I am mortally afraid of earthquakes."

George laughed.

"Look, it's not funny, George."

"I'm sorry."

Mollified, she added, "And besides, Uncle Percy needs us."

"It suited you. You wanted to get away from Don Diamond."

"All right, I did want to get away from Don, but Uncle Percy was kind to my mother. When my father died and she started all that traveling from one place to another, she told me it was Uncle Percy who would send her a dollar or two when she was really broke. No one else did. Speaking of which, how much money have you got?"

"Twenty bucks."

"I'll have to ask Uncle Percy for some more." She thought of Uncle Percy's hollering. "But perhaps not today. We'll manage somehow."

"Doritos," he said as he chewed on his waffle, "and waffles."

"Doritos," she said and added them to her list.

"You could have left me behind."

"On your own? In a trailer park? With your lousy friends? Not a chance. Salsa."

"What am I going to do here? Who am I going to meet?"

"You can go back to school."

"I'm finished with school."

"You can learn a trade. You can get a job."

"Sure. Sweeping floors. Cleaning windows."

"Those are jobs."

"I don't want them."

"Then learn a trade if you're so smart. Besides, we need the money."

George got up and went to the door and looked out through the back porch. It was a beautiful day, the air clear and cold and the leaves on the maple trees just beginning to turn red and gold. But something else had caught his eye. Actually, it was impossible to miss.

"Hey, have you seen this?"

"What?" Joelene came to the door and opened it. The back porch had been glassed in since she was a girl. But half of it was in darkness now because outside, looming three stories high, was a—a structure.

"What the hell is that?" said George, stepping down from the porch and staring up at it.

"I think it's—an ark," said Joelene, coming out and

standing beside him. They both gaped up at it. Joelene put up her hand to shield her eyes as though she were looking up at a mountaintop.

"Oh, my, my, my," she said. It was not the kind of thing you expected to find in someone's back yard.

It loomed above them, the walls smooth as cliffs. The walls were sixty feet high and stretched two hundred feet from the back of the house to the end of Uncle Percy's yard, where the woods rose away on a hill.

Joelene had never seen anything like it. It dwarfed her. It made her feel like an ant foraging below an enormous porcelain bowl. She went closer and the wall bulged out above her and she had to put her hand out to steady herself against the narrowing keel.

"It's a goddam ship!" said George.

"No. It's an ark," said Joelene. " 'Make thee an ark of gopher wood.' "

"Holy cow!" said George.

The wood, whatever it was, had weathered to a silvery gray. It reminded Joelene of the skin of a shark she had once seen at the San Diego aquarium. The skin had seemed old, ancient as the sea the shark had swum in. The wood of the ark seemed like that. The ark was not new.

Joelene and George walked around the whole perimeter, stepping through and over the scaffolding that supported it. The scaffolding itself was massive, and George swung on it and whooped and scratched under his armpit as he hung from one beam and swung over another.

Wood shavings and piles of old sawdust were everywhere. Under a canvas lean-to was a workbench, a lathe, planing tools, a vise; a few odd tools looked as though they had just been set down: a hammer, chisel, rasps, and so forth. There was a stack of planks, all neat and trimmed. George kept whistling as they walked around and took in the size of the project.

"I always liked woodworking in high school," said George.

"There's no way in," said Joelene, but George spied a low door, flush as a seal on a Ziploc bag, and pried it open with a crowbar. Then he propped the door open with a brick.

Joelene stepped inside, and when her eyes got used to the change in light the interior took her breath away.

"Oh, my, my, my," she said again and sat down on a wooden trestle.

"Christ," said George and sat down beside her.

The interior soared away from them, bursting to the sky like some Gothic cathedral. At the very top the ark was open and the oval of the sky glowed down on them like a Buddha's eye. Although the exterior wood had been gray, gray as the sea, the wood inside seemed as fresh as an evergreen forest beside a lake. Every surface shone and glistened as though it had been freshly polished. The surfaces were gilded or muted depending on how the sunlight hit them. Even the dust motes sparkled in the air.

Joelene thought of a miniature painting she had once

seen in a museum. She thought that just as the details of the miniature had been too obscure to be seen by the naked eye, so too she could not see the dusky edges of the ark. And yet she knew, she remembered, that when she had raised the magnifying glass to her eye, the hidden details were revealed, hair stroke by hair stroke, and Joelene knew that Uncle Percy's ark, explored step by step, would reveal the same painstaking, loving care.

The ribs of the ark were carved and planed, and no surface or strut was without a curve, a scroll, a curlicue. Three stories or decks curved around the bulging walls of the ark, but there was no feeling of enclosure or claustrophobia here in the deepest part of the hull. Instead, there was a glorious feeling of being in a bud, a large bud, one that would swell and burst open to the promise of the space above it.

Joelene and George sat on the trestle dumbstruck and tried to take it all in. Joelene saw there was a staircase that spiraled up past the three partial decks to the sky. The cheeks of the stairs were carved to resemble waves like those on a Japanese print, and rope—thick white rope—was plied, woven, knotted, and threaded through brass loops to form the balusters, spindles, and rails.

It was the most beautiful staircase Joelene had ever seen, and she had read a lot of *Architectural Digest*s. Joelene stood up. The staircase exerted an irresistible urge to be climbed. Joelene forgot about her phobia of heights, but no sooner had she crossed to it and placed one hand on the rope than a rifle shot rang out above her head. Joelene screamed and George hit the floor. Another shot whined above them.

"Take one more step and it'll be the last you ever do." Uncle Percy's voice rang out in the huge space.

"Why, you scared me, Uncle Percy!" said Joelene, turning to face him. Her face was white in the gloom. "Where are you? I can't even see you."

"Near the door. You both come over here right now."

George uncovered his head and rolled over.

"We've got a loony for an uncle," he said as he stepped across the floor toward the door.

Joelene was shaking like the rope she had touched, but her fear gave her courage. "I am mad as hell," she said as she reached Uncle Percy. "You put George and me in danger." Uncle Percy just gave her his gimlet eye as he stood propped against the doorway with the gun in his hands. "You had no need to scare me half to death and practically kill us. You could have asked us to leave, just ask us, but no, you—"

"Shut up, woman," said Uncle Percy. Little beads of sweat had broken out on his forehead with the effort of standing there and discharging the rifle. The sweat caused his eyeglasses to slip down his nose.

"I will not shut up," said Joelene, walking past him with her head in the air. "And the name is Joelene. I was curious, that's all." She stepped out of the ark without looking back.

Uncle Percy began to sway and his arms dropped as George reached him. George put out a steadying hand. "Come on, Percy," he said, taking his weight.

"Close the goddam door," whispered Uncle Percy, all his strength gone as they stepped outside. He was mumbling, " 'A window shalt thou make . . . and in a cubit shalt thou finish it above. . . .' " George kicked the brick away and half carried, half dragged Uncle Percy back into the house.

The phone was ringing in the hallway. It was the only phone in the house. Joelene snatched it off the hook.

"Hello?"

A man's voice said, "Is that Joelene Mathieson speaking?"

"Yes. Who's this?"

The phone clicked and the dial tone came on.

"Hello?" said Joelene. After a moment she shrugged and hung up. She came back into the kitchen to get her list and her car keys. She was still shaking from being shot at. She looked at Uncle Percy warily.

"I'm going over to the supermarket. Anything special you want?"

Uncle Percy sat exhausted at the kitchen table. His eyes seemed even larger in his face than usual. His thin frame shook under his pajamas. Joelene knelt down beside him.

"We shouldn't have pried. I didn't know it was so important."

"The door was shut," he said. "There are no doorknobs for a reason. It's to keep nosy people out."

George and Joelene glanced at each other. George said nothing, and Joelene got up and put on her thin white jacket. Her lips had got thin too.

"Well, don't worry about us, Uncle Percy. I never stay anywhere more than a few days, weeks if I like it. That's it. Ask George. No wonder he doesn't do well at school. How many has it been, George, ten? Twenty?"

"Seventeen."

Joelene applied some pink lipstick, using the glass upper half of the door as her mirror.

"Seventeen. S-e-v-e-n-t-e-e-n." She screwed the lipstick back into its case. "But that's what made America great. Move on. Hit the highway. If things don't work out, move on again. There's work down in Hootsville, or Flagstaff, or Sulphur Springs. 'Do you know they're looking for a waitress thirty miles up the road on Route 101?' Pack the baby in the wagon. Leave the icebox to defrost. Don't look so down in the mouth, there, George. You have never gone hungry because of me. Look at your general knowledge. You're a whiz at *Jeopardy!* You know, one of these days I'm going to get you on that show. 'American Money for four hundred dollars. The structure seen on the back of the currently minted nickel.' "

"What is Monticello?" said George despondently.

"Ri-i-ight," said Joelene, squeezing his chin. "See what I mean?"

"Mom, get off it," said George, pushing away her

hand. Uncle Percy sat at the table brooding.

"Well, I have to go shopping," said Joelene. "I hope they accept my bank card. George, put a coat on Uncle Percy." She slammed the door and left.

"She's upset," said George.

"I need to finish it," said Uncle Percy.

"Finish what?" George had absentmindedly picked up a small jack plane from outside the door. He ran his hand over the smooth handle. It fitted nicely into the soft part of his palm.

"My work," said Uncle Percy. He watched George handling the plane. "I could show you how to do it. You could help me. Here. Git my coat." With an amazing show of strength he stood up by himself. "And my shoes."

"Nah. Mom will kill me."

"Look, boy. I don't have much time. If pew-monia don't get me, my heart will. You know what it's like to work for years on something and not be able to finish it? No, how could you?"

George didn't answer.

"Women don't know," said Uncle Percy. "They don't know what a man has to do."

George looked uncomfortable. Uncle Percy leaned over the table till he was staring George right in the eye.

"Have you ever wanted to do something so bad the fear of hell wouldn't stop you?" said Uncle Percy.

"Yeah, a Grateful Dead concert. Mom wouldn't let me go."

"And?"

"I went."

"And?"

"Nothing happened."

"And now? What do you want most now?"

"I want to go back to California."

"Well, I can help you." Uncle Percy's scrawny hand gripped George's suddenly like a vise. "If you'll help me."

"How?"

"I'll give you the money for a ticket. I don't want you here neither."

"Help you how?"

"Help me finish my ark."

"No gun?"

"No gun. Put it under my bed. Git my coat."

"I think I'm going to regret this," said George, loping off to the bedroom. He hesitated at the door of Uncle Percy's room, changed his mind, and took the gun, unloaded it, and placed it above the lace cover on the four-poster bed in his mother's room. If you looked real close you could see it, but Uncle Percy wouldn't. George felt better knowing Uncle Percy couldn't get his hands on it.

He went to get a coat. "And bring my toolbox," shouted Uncle Percy. "It's behind the door." George could hardly lift the red metal box. He struggled out with it to the kitchen, banging it painfully against his legs. "Put it in the ark," said Uncle Percy, "just inside the door." George did so and came back to Uncle Percy, who had begun making his own way down the steps. He was using his walking sticks and, although painful to watch, he moved easier than he had the day before with his walker.

"Will this thing really sail?" said George.

"You don't have to sail to get where I'm going," said Uncle Percy. He stopped for breath at the door of the ark, and George helped him step over the threshold. When he looked around the ark, Uncle Percy's face lit up like it was glowing from inside. He smiled so that his teeth and lips disappeared. He looked like a gnome in his striped pajamas and torn green anorak. Then he did the tortoise thing with his neck and said, "George, go and get that jack plane you had in the kitchen."

"I can't leave you in here."

Uncle Percy snarled. "Jist do it."

George took off reluctantly. He got to the bottom of the back porch steps when he heard the door of the ark slam shut.

"Uncle Percy?" George ran back to the ark. He could hear Uncle Percy hammering away inside, nailing the door shut.

"Let me in," he shouted, angered. "How can I help you if you won't let me in?"

He threw his shoulder against the door, but Uncle Percy kept hammering away and laughing. George looked for the crowbar, but he had left it inside the ark.

It was hopeless trying to break in. George slumped down against the wooden wall. "You'll be sorry!" he shouted. "You'll have to come out some time." There was no reply from inside, just a shuffling noise, and then even that faded away. George pressed his ear against the wall but could hear nothing. He examined his sandals for a while and the edges of his frayed jeans. He played with the woven bands on his wrists. He whistled a few bars of his latest bootleg tape. He pulled his jacket tighter. The blue sky and the sun had gone and it was cold. Suddenly George was hungry. He loped into the house and made himself a sandwich with some stale cheese and mayo. He filled a mug with coffee and took it outside and hunkered down again against the door into the ark.

Uncle Percy had to come out this way. He would get tired and cold. He'd get hungry. George chewed on a bit of rind. Curse the old man, he thought. Curse his mother. He could be lying on the beach at Malibu listening to music instead of sitting here freezing to death. George shifted his weight from one bony haunch to the other. He searched his jacket for a joint, but the pockets were empty. Joelene, he thought. He took out his Walkman, plugged it into his ears, and settled back to wait.

"Thank you for using AT and T."

"Hello, boss? It's me, Ernie."

"Did you find her?"

"Yeah. She's here, all right."

"Is the car there?"

"I can't see the car."

"What d'ya mean you can't see the car? She drove there, didn't she?"

"The car's not here. Honest. I been sitting outside in the friggin' cold opposite the house and it ain't there."

"Ernie, it's kinda hard to miss, isn't it—a bright orange Mustang with a black top? It's twenty-five years old, Ernie!"

"Boss, I know cars. It ain't here this morning. There's a truck, a blue Chevy, belongs to the old man—"

"I don't want to hear about the old man's truck. I want the car. Now don't call me again unless you've got good news."

Brrrrrrrrrrrr.

"She-e-it."

Joelene drove her bright orange Mustang with the black top over to the supermarket at the mall. She had the window down because the air was so fresh and clean. When the car worked, she liked driving it. She liked the way the engine responded to her foot on the pedal. The car kind of floated in the front because the steering was loose, but she liked that too because she was used to it. Joelene floated to a stop at a traffic light and was aware of the covetous glances of some young dudes in a pickup beside her. They revved their engine. Joelene kept her eyes to the front. Joelene, she said to herself, you are not a kid anymore. She cranked the window up and the knob fell off. Then the light began to change and the kids revved their engine again and Joelene could not resist the challenge. Down went her foot and—*pow*—off she took, leaving the smell of burnt rubber and black marks on the asphalt and the dudes still standing at the light as she streaked away.

"Why, you must be Joelene's boy. George, isn't it?"

It was hours later and the sun had gone in and it had started to snow. My mother, my sister, and I stood looking down at George. My mother is rather large but she has a pretty face.

"I'm Moira," she said, "and these are my daughters, Gerry and Ondine."

George scrambled to his feet, or rather he unfolded his long, stiff legs and poked out his arms and shrugged his hair back and grinned at us. He looked really goofy. I saw my mother looking at his earring.

"Hey," said Gerry. "Anyone ever tell you that you look like Tommy Tune?"

"Hush, Geraldine," said Moira. "Where are your manners?" She turned to George. "We thought we might pop in and see how you and Joelene are getting on. Everything is all right, isn't it?"

"Hi. Sure. Fine."

"Where *is* Joelene? Why are you sitting outside?"

"Um, Mom's gone to do some shopping. She'll be back soon."

George began ushering us back to the house. But Moira stood with her booted feet planted firmly, looking up at the soaring bulwarks.

"I see you've been admiring the ark. Poor Uncle Percy. Every penny of his Social Security has gone into this for the past twenty years. I don't know where it will all end."

"Where *is* Uncle Percy?" said Gerry. She snapped some gum with her teeth.

"I'm—not sure right now."

Just then we heard a steady whupping sound from inside the ark. The whupping got louder and faster as though a winch was suddenly running out of control and a cable was snapping out its length. Then there was a loud thud, which shook the ground, and a faint "Help!"—which sounded as if it reached us from the other end of a tunnel and which we all recognized as the voice of Uncle Percy.

"Boy, are you in trouble," I said.

"Oh, no," said Moira, putting her hands on her hips and looking accusingly at George. "You let him in the ark, didn't you?"

"I couldn't help it."

Moira shook her chestnut hair and swung into action.

"You keep talking to him. I'll go and call Pete at the firehouse." Moira went off with her hips shaking like a hula dancer under her brown polyester slacks. She looks better from the front. "This is the third time since Labor Day that they've had to rescue him."

We soon heard the siren, and then the fire truck pulled up in front of the house and a group of men led by Pete came around the corner with their axes and ladders and hooks.

"Yeah, we figured," said Pete, listening to Moira and motioning two burly men to start breaking down the door. It soon lay in splinters, and after they yanked back the last plank they all trooped inside and hollered for Uncle Percy. Somewhere in the gloom a small generator was working and a series of pulleys and ropes moved laboriously around a set of winches.

"There he is," said Gerry, pointing upward. In the soft blue light of the sifting afternoon snow they saw Uncle Percy dangling upside down in midair.

"Oh, my God," said Moira.

"Are you all right, Percy?" Pete shouted through his cupped hands.

" 'Course I'm all right," Percy shouted back. He swung around in slow arcs, his right leg caught in the loop of a suspended rope. "Right as any damn fool could be swingin' upside down on the end of a rope. Git me out of here!"

"Oh, Lordy," said Moira. "His heart. Be careful."

"Moira," said Pete, "if this doesn't kill your uncle, nothing will." He set off up the stairs with his grappling hooks.

"Merciful Being," said Joelene's voice from the doorway as she came onto the scene. "What are you doing up there, Pericles Morgan? I go out for an hour's shopping and I come back and there's a fire truck blinking and winking in the driveway, there are people gawking and cars everywhere—oh, hello, Moira—and where do I find you? Not in bed, not sitting down, but hanging by one leg sixty feet above the ground like some damn fool circus performer."

"I ain't gonna listen to you, woman," said Uncle Percy, crossing his arms across his chest.

"Oh, yes, you will," said Joelene, starting up the stairs and climbing up to his eye level. "Excuse me," she said, passing Pete on the stairs.

"Hi, I'm Pete."

Joelene ignored him, which is difficult to do because he's a tall, strong guy with a big black mustache. She shouted across at her uncle's red face.

"Now listen here, you gimlet-eyed little gnome. I dropped everything in California to come here to look after you. I don't get paid for this. I don't expect anything in return but some common decency. But what happens? I'm freezing to death in this wretched house. There's mice eating potatoes under my bed at night. The checkout girl won't take my bank card without a fight.

I get shot at. You spit my food on the floor. And now you almost hang yourself working on this infernal machine. And half the town is standing in the yard to see what stupid blamed thing you're going to do next. Who needs this? I surely don't."

Uncle Percy swayed across her vision, and Joelene realized that she was way above ground level. She felt dizzy and tried to fix her eyes on Uncle Percy's face. But Uncle Percy had shut his eyes and opened his mouth.

"Deliver me, O Lord, from my enemies. Let them not be victorious against me." He swung himself in a loop and tightened his arms across his chest. His voice was strong. "Make their threats against me fall back on them. Let them return from whence they came."

"Excuse me, ma'am, I have to have room to work," said Pete. He took Joelene's shoulders in his hands and moved her down a step.

"Men," said Joelene, tossing her shoulders and marching down the stairs. "George, come into the kitchen. I want to talk to you."

As George went by, following his mother, Gerry smiled at him. "He's cute," she said to me.

Moira followed George out the door. "I can't bear to watch this," she said.

"I think it's kind of fun," said Gerry. "It's always so dull around here."

I ran home to get my camera.

Three

I'm fourteen. I'm smart, but I'm pretty ugly. I believe I have inherited the same head knobs as Uncle Percy. Phrenology is something I'm interested in, but not with myself as the subject. No one takes me seriously, though. Particularly not my mother. When I told her I was running away from home once, she packed my bag for me. She knew I wouldn't leave. And another time when I complained about an outbreak on my face and said I really should see a dermatologist and Mindy Moston's dermatologist had given her a mint face mask, she went out and bought me a mask too—except mine was from the Halloween store.

I'm Gerry's younger sister, Ondine. No one takes any notice of me. I'm kind of invisible. You know, I sit there and people forget I'm still listening. Like the time Moira talked about Joelene's problems with George and marijuana? My mom is the only person who still calls pot "mariwhuana." I thought it was a new girlfriend of George's she was talking about until I caught on. You pick up interesting stuff if you just keep quiet and listen.

When Moira had us she was going through a phase of naming kids with "-ine" on the end. Geraldine. Ondine. Pauline. (She's eleven, prepubescent, no zits yet.) Moira worked in a bookstore once, which probably explains something.

What you have to remember is that all the Morgans have a religious streak. That probably explains something too. In some it's a liberating experience, I guess. My grandfather, Alexander, who was Uncle Percy's uncle, was an Episcopalian missionary. He worked and traveled in the islands of the Pacific. My dad says he got involved in some kind of cargo cult and to this day there are still natives who worship him as Alexander Frum. He was known as Alexander from America, see, but maybe Dad's only pulling my leg.

In others, like Mom, religion can be a bummer. I'd like just once to see Mom kick up her heels or whatever old folks do. I mean she's so predictable. And Uncle Percy—now, he's another one. He can spout the Old and New Testaments until the cows come home, but he swears like a trouper and I don't know when was the last time he came to church with us. There's something in Uncle Percy's past that no one talks about but everyone knows. I hate it when adults do that. I don't know what it is. But one day they'll just blurt it out and I'll be there listening. Dad says listening is a great skill in a journalist, which is what I want to be. Mom says it's a great skill in anyone, but Dad didn't hear her.

When I returned to Uncle Percy's house with my camera it was like all hell had broken loose. There were a number of cars parked randomly along the street. The minibus the retarded people use was abandoned halfway across their driveway. They live at the Peter Pan Community Home, which is the big house, the one with the dormer windows, one up from Uncle Percy's. Two or three of them holding hands waved to me as I went by on my bike. Some of them have that mongoloid look. I waved back. They're like big kids, really. Parrish is my favorite. He looks Japanese.

The fire truck had churned up the whole driveway at Uncle Percy's, and the snow was just slush and mud. Moira and Joelene had called an ambulance, as Uncle Percy had turned a strange blue color, and the neighbors were still around, all gawking and chattering. Gerry's boyfriend, Mike Astanazy, who washes dishes at the diner, had arrived on his motorbike. My dad doesn't like him. Mike was outside revving up his secondhand Yamaha. He'd really like to have a Harley-Davidson. He thinks he's cool; he's not.

There were one or two kids hanging around Joelene's orange Mustang. It's the color of a persimmon. The top is black and it has duct tape holding on the back window.

It must be a gas guzzler like my dad says. Thirteen miles to the gallon and only takes premium. Dad's a supervisor at the tollbooths on the Thruway, so he sees a lot of cars. He says the Mustang is just the kind of impractical car that Joelene would have. He says she should have a little Nissan or even a Hyundai. *That* she could afford. Everyone seems to know that Joelene is broke except Joelene.

"Honey," she said to George, as I entered the kitchen, "can you bring in the last bag of groceries?" She had coffee and Sara Lee cinnamon rolls hot from the oven sitting on paper towels on the kitchen table. My mother never has Sara Lee. She bakes from scratch. She has never been seen to crack open a frozen roll of croissant dough; she rubs fat into flour with her fingertips. She never uses paper towels either.

All the firemen were there. They are all volunteers but they do a great job. In summer they have regular meetings in the firehouse and hold practice drills. We all hang over the yard fences slapping mayflies and watching them run for their cars when the siren goes. At Halloween they turn the upstairs of the firehouse into a party room for us kids. They even have fireworks. On Christmas Eve we run an extension cord from the firehouse across the road to the maple tree in the square and plug in the fairy lights and sing carols. Then Miss Avery, the schoolteacher who has a crush on Pete on account of his mustache, brings out chocolate chip cookies. But the oldies usually leave us and rush into Pool's place for beer and brandy. They all get real drunk.

Anyway, there was Pete, who really runs the local insurance agency; Buddy, who owns the garage but spends most of his time sleeping or fishing; Pool Jarvis, who is the bartender at the Inn and mows people's lawns for six-fifty an hour on Saturdays, and Lars, who looks after the stables and generally caretakes for the rich who come up here from New York to "get away from everything" and "get back to nature" and employ people like Lars to make sure they don't. Also digging in were two paramedics who had "stabilized" Uncle Percy and declared he did not need to go to the hospital. Uncle Percy was back in his own bed, with a couple of bricks under the headboard to help him breathe and a Valium in his milk to help him relax. He'd need it if he woke up and found all these people eating his grub in his kitchen.

George went out to the car with Gerry in tow. The waiting Yamaha made a roar as Gerry appeared.

"Hey," shouted Mike to George. "Anyone ever tell you you look like Ichabod Crane?"

"Dope," said Parrish. Parrish may be retarded, but he's smarter than a lot of people.

George smiled and loped over to his mother's car and opened the trunk. He had to use the keys to open it. The next few things happened quickly. A man in an LA Lakers jacket came running up the street, pushed George into the trunk of the Mustang, and slammed the lid. He grabbed the keys from the lock, shoved Gerry aside, threw himself into the car, started it, and drove off in reverse with the tires squealing. It all happened so fast no one knew what was happening until Gerry started screaming and everyone ran out of the kitchen, along the hall, and onto the front porch.

"Where's my car?" shouted Joelene, as Pete took in the situation and radioed the state troopers.

"They've taken George," said Gerry and burst into tears.

The Yamaha did a wheelie as Mike spun off down the road in pursuit of the Mustang.

"Why would anyone steal George?" said Joelene.

The fire truck took off too, with the men clinging to the sides. Dusk was coming in early, and the snow swirled softly in the headlights. The ambulance left and people drifted away.

"Come inside," said Moira, putting her arms around Joelene's shoulders. She felt Joelene's thinness through her thin blouse. "Honey, you need some warm clothes in this climate."

"George is really a good boy," said Joelene, blinking under the harsh kitchen light.

When a mother says this you know she's about to tell you all the things that are bad.

"He's young and silly. I know he's lazy and dropped out of school. He got kicked out really for smoking pot. I know he lies to me. But he's looked after me. When his father died, it was George who helped me over it. He used to put on a pair of Tom's shoes and a hat and pretend he was the man of the house." Joelene acted this out by lowering her voice and sticking her stomach out. She laughed. "And then when the quake hit . . . it was George who got me out of the house seconds before the roof caved in." Joelene snapped her fingers. "Seconds."

"Sit down," said Moira. "Have a cup of coffee."

"All we had left was Tom's car and the clothes we stood in. We were just getting on our feet. I'd planted some bougainvillea in the garden." Joelene began to cry. Moira tsked in sympathy. "I got a job as a secretary and bookkeeper at an auto showroom. Don Diamond's on Sepulveda?" She raised her voice like it was a question, as if Moira might recognize the name. "Everything was going fine until—uh, Don and I got romantically interested in each other." Joelene looked up quickly at her cousin and then got up and pulled some paper tissues from a box. She blew her nose loudly. "That was a big mistake." Joelene went to the sink and splashed water on her face. "Enough of this sentimentality," she said. "It gets one nowhere." She took a yellow gummy bear from a white paper bag on the countertop and chewed it mournfully.

"I do admire you, Joelene," said Moira. "You've got more pluck than a chicken." Moira's metaphors are sometimes hard to grasp. "And you're such a little bitty thing, too."

Joelene began clearing away the coffee things. "I'm

going to cook something for supper while I'm waiting to hear. I bought a whole stack of frozen dinners. You three want to stay?"

The phone rang and Joelene ran into the hallway to answer it. "Oh, thank God." She hung up, her face beaming. "They've found George. He was hitchhiking on the Thruway, trying to get back. They're driving him home."

"And the car?"

"No sign yet. But who cares? It's George I was worried about."

"We should be getting home," said Moira. "Call us if you need us. Come on, girls. Your father will be starving and his shift starts soon."

Gerry clapped her hand over her mouth. "I forgot all about work, what with the excitement and all. My boss'll kill me."

"No, he won't," I said. "His dishwasher is here, too." The faithful Yamaha and its warrior had returned. Mike sat on his bike under a street lamp as though he were resting. He revved up his bike when he saw Gerry and fastened his chin strap; otherwise he gave no sign of recognition. He's so gross. Gerry hesitated for a second, then slipped onto the pillion and put on the spare helmet. Women are so weak, I thought, as they roared away.

Four

The next morning Joelene was applying salve to the rope burn on Uncle Percy's leg. She had been up for hours and had already added to her file on household hints a new clipping from the *Times*—how to regrout a tiled bathroom. She had begun the morning by clearing out the cabinets in the kitchen and had lined the shelves with fresh newspaper. That's how she had seen the article on grouting.

Outside on either side of the house she had walked the wooden verandas and lifted the plastic sheets that covered old garden pots and a rusted swing seat she vaguely remembered seeing her mother swing on, long ago. It had a fringed top and faded yellow roses on the cushions. She had found a door off the kitchen that hid a narrow staircase, and she had gone upstairs and explored the abandoned rooms that Uncle Percy never used. Then she had taken down and washed and dried the curtains in the kitchen.

Uncle Percy's bedroom window faced the front garden and had a view of the street. Bright sunshine poured across the lawn, and the wind stirred the red leaves of the maple tree. The snow of the day before was melting; it dripped profuse and sparkling from the eaves and the branches and puddled in the thick piles of fallen leaves.

"How do you feel?" asked Joelene, applying a bandage and pulling down Uncle Percy's pajama leg.

"Lousy."

She laughed. "Well, at least that's honest."

Uncle Percy cricked his neck from one side to the other. "I feel like my neck's broke."

"Then turn around and I'll massage it."

Uncle Percy hesitated. "You can't get around me like that. I know women's ways."

Joelene sighed and began tidying up a pile of bills and letters and empty tobacco pouches and cigarette papers and large maroon-edged handkerchiefs still in their cellophane wrappings from the bedside table.

"And don't go messing with my things."

"I'm just trying to help."

"Stealing from me."

Joelene burst into tears. "I'm not stealing from you. I wouldn't stay here if I had somewhere else to go."

Uncle Percy's hands began clawing through his bedside drawer. Joelene blew her nose and shoved the tissue back in her jeans pocket. "What are you looking for?"

"My wallet. Someone took it. Damn buggers."

"No one took it. What does it look like?"

"Green."

Joelene's eyes swiveled around the room as she began to search. She found the old green wallet in a plastic butter dish under a pile of clothes on a chair and handed it to him triumphantly. "Uncle Percy, you'd save yourself a lot of grief if you'd let me tidy this mess up for you. No wonder you can't find anything."

Uncle Percy lay back against his pillows, hugging his green wallet to his chest.

"I know where my things are. Don't go touching things."

But Joelene had knelt on the floor and was rifling through a box of bills and documents and old keys and photographs. "Like this," she said. "Here's a prescription for your medicine. You never filled it. Or this—or this." Joelene held up three little books and laughed. "Uncle Percy, you've got three different bankbooks here."

"Give me those," he said. He smiled cunningly. "I don't pay taxes anymore. I hate the IRS. They'll never get another cent from me."

"If you don't sort it out they'll get it all in the end anyway. Nobody else will." But she was concentrating on the photographs in the box, photographs that were thirty, forty years old: Percy as a young man; Percy with his father; Percy and Arthur swinging axes in the lumberyard. There was a big wooden sign above them that read *Morgan Lumberyard* in prosperous-looking script.

"What happened to the lumberyard?" said Joelene.

"Couldn't make a go of it."

"And look at this. Here's a photo of my mother." The photograph had been scissored in two. Joelene stood up and handed it to him and, as she did so, saw over his bony head her Mustang turning into the driveway followed by a state trooper's car.

"Well, heavens," she said, "they've found my car." She left Uncle Percy with the photograph and went to the front porch. She recognized Pete at the wheel as he struggled to open the door. He was wearing a gray business suit and a brown felt Stetson.

"Jiggle the handle," she said. "It always sticks. Where did you find it?"

"On the highway. It had run out of gas."

"I didn't have enough money with me to fill it up yesterday."

"There's no damage as far as I can see. But this is an unusual car around here. You'd be better locking it up."

"I'll keep it in the garage in future. Half the time it doesn't go anyway. I spent eight hundred dollars on a new transmission last month."

Pete had taken off his Stetson and wiped his hand up across his brow. He smiled at her.

"You got insurance?"

"Yes." She laughed.

"How's George this morning?"

"He's still sleeping it off."

"And Percy?"

"Sore."

Pete stood with one foot in the open door of the police car. He seemed reluctant to leave.

"If there's anything I can do to help—or, you know, if George wants something to do—give me a call. He said he might like to see what we do on fire drills."

"Thanks. I will."

They drove off and Joelene went to investigate the garage, which was dwarfed by the shadow of the ark. The wooden doors were badly warped and squeaked loudly as she dragged them open. The garage was jammed with belongings. It was like an attic, full of boxes and shelves, bottles and wooden doors, a lawn mower, broken furniture, plastic bins, trunks, household poisons, bags of garden fertilizers and potting soil, a wheelbarrow, old kitchen chairs, a workbench hidden under more bottles and boxes. Joelene groaned. There was hardly room for one car, let alone two. Uncle Percy was constitutionally incapable of throwing anything away.

"What are you doing, Mom?" George stood silhouetted against the open door.

"Oh, good, you're up and dressed. How are you feeling?" Joelene hauled a box of books out into the sunshine.

"I'm fine. What are you doing?"

"I'm making room for the car."

"I'll do it."

Joelene straightened up with surprise. "You will?"

"Yeah, I'll do it. Don't you worry about a thing."

"You feeling all right, George?" She put a hand on his forehead. "Did you get bumped on the head last night?"

George looked genuinely hurt.

"OK," said Joelene, holding up her hands in surrender. "I'll leave you to it. Thanks." She shook her head in amazement as she went back into the house.

Uncle Percy was no longer in his bed. He was in the kitchen, sitting at the table grinding coffee beans.

"Cain't stand that powdered stuff," he said.

Between his bony knees he held a small wooden coffee grinder, and he slowly wound the handle around. Periodically he would stop and shake it and inspect the drawer to see if it was full.

"I remember you doing that when I was a girl," said Joelene. "You did it just the same way."

"Same grinder," said Uncle Percy. He tipped the coffee carefully into the basket of a small aluminum coffeepot, added a pinch of salt, and replaced the lid. A large button was wired onto the lid in place of a knob. Joelene put the pot on the stove, and soon a cheerful perking sound filled the kitchen.

"I've worked out your housekeeping money," said Uncle Percy, pointing to a small mound of notes and coins weighted down by a screwdriver. His green wallet lay on the table. Joelene had told him earlier that she had had to borrow from the jar.

"I need that," said Joelene. "I spent sixty-four dollars yesterday."

"Sixty-four dollars!" Uncle Percy's mouth dropped open in disbelief. "I cain't afford that."

"I can't feed us on less."

Uncle Percy's head dropped into his hands. "Sixty-four dollars," he whispered. "That's more'n fourteen pounds of screws. Ten yards of rope." He looked up at Joelene. "That's enough for a Black and Decker reversible drill and two pints of oil!"

"But we can't eat those, Uncle Percy. I can't make s-o-u-p from a stone." She got up from the table and poured him a cup of coffee. There were no small spoons so she handed him a sundae spoon.

"And don't go on with that spellin' game neither," he said. "I never was keen on book learning."

"Neither is George," she said, joining him with a second cup, "and he's got a photographic memory. But my mother and I loved games. My, how she loved words! She would have made a great teacher. She was always writing letters, letters to the editor or complaints to the Water Board or the Highway Department." Joelene giggled.

"Damn busybody."

"Oh, Uncle Percy, she couldn't help it. She was so—

so intelligent, so frustrated. She worked as a waitress, not that there's anything wrong with that. It was hard work and she was good at it. She worked as a maid at motels. She was a switchboard operator once. Don't know what happened to that job. Boise, I think it was." Joelene sipped her coffee. "Delicious! But boy, did she love words! Every time we'd move to a new place, out would come the Scrabble board. It was the first thing we unpacked. I loved the little shiny tiles in the soft pouch and trying to get to the triple word scores in the corners."

Uncle Percy growled but Joelene took no notice.

"My mother used to do it—spell things out when I was small so I wouldn't understand. Like when she couldn't pay the rent? And then it became a game, 'Come on, honey, it's time to p-a-c-k. Let's tiptoe out so no one hears us.' "

Joelene stopped and stared into her cup.

"I thought Tom and I would be together in one place forever. He was going to build me a house with bougainvillea all over it and impatiens in the borders. He was going to make a million dollars one day, he said. He used to talk about it in his sleep. The big time. And then he died and there was nothing. He didn't even have insurance."

"I have to finish my boat," said Uncle Percy, getting up from the table.

"When you're stronger."

"I ain't got time to wait." Uncle Percy slammed his hand down on the table so the cups jumped.

"Hey, Mom," said George, coming into the kitchen, "this is Parrish from the house down the road. He's going to help me clean out the garage."

Parrish hesitated at the door. Uncle Percy growled.

"Come in, come in," said Joelene.

"Hide your things," grumped Uncle Percy, picking up his green wallet.

Parrish blushed and stepped in and took off his red-peaked hat. His smile had the innocence of an angel. His hair was straight, black and shiny and cut in a bowl shape, and he was about thirty years old with the mind of a child.

"Hi," said Joelene, shaking hands. Parrish looked at his sneakers.

"He says he saw the man who took the car yesterday. He'd been hanging around all day."

"Was it the same man you saw?"

"It was too dark to see him when he let me out of the trunk. He just kicked me and told me to take off. I did."

"I like bathketball," said Parrish.

"Sneakin' around," said Uncle Percy. "You stay off my land, you and your friends, you hear?" He got up and stumped toward the door.

George placed himself between Uncle Percy and his new friend. They began to walk sideways to the back door.

"The sooner we get the car into the garage, the better," said George.

Uncle Percy stopped suddenly. "What car? What garage?" He stumped as rapidly as he could back across the kitchen and stared down at the garage from the window. A lifetime of squirreled belongings already stood outside in the sunshine. He took a deep gasp of air through his open mouth.

"Uncle Percy," said Joelene, "there's no need to get so excited. We'll put everything back when we get the car in."

Uncle Percy's mouth shut like a clam. He pulled his head into his shoulders, swung around without a word, and stumped to his room and slammed the door.

"Oh, dear," said Joelene. "I hate confrontation. Come on, George, Parrish. Let's get the car in and everything back before he has a heart attack." They rushed outside. Uncle Percy's voice followed them. They could hear him crashing about in his room, and Joelene winced every time she heard something fall. But his voice went on.

"If I'd wanted a woman in the house I'da hired a housekeeper. Women can't stay out of things. Damn buggers. Where did they put my whiskey? Changin' everythin'. I had it organized jist the way I like. The way I like it, nobody else. Spendin' my money. Sixty-four dollars! Leavin' lights on. Puttin' up the furnace. Woman wants to live in bloody *Florida* and here we are in Poe-kipsie. You could get a suntan in here she's got so many damn lights on. *Put the lights off!* Cleanin' out my garage. Look at that. She's puttin' her car in the garage and my truck outside. Look at those pigeons, droppin' crap on my winder." Uncle Percy rapped the window with his walking stick. *"Get those birds offen my truck!* Damn buggers."

Everyone was exhausted by the end of the day. Uncle Percy's rage had finally subsided and he fell into a fitful sleep after refusing his lunch. At four o'clock Joelene took him his medicine and a cup of buttermilk, which he swallowed in one gulp. But he wouldn't speak and he shut his eyes when she tried to talk to him. Joelene ached all over from bending and stretching and lifting and hauling. George was still outside with Parrish.

"Want to thee thomething?" said Parrish.

"Sure, man. What's up?"

Parrish led the way through the scaffolding to the woods behind the ark. They had to climb up the slope a little way and step over the remains of old dry stone walls. Bracken and scrub grew thickly under the trees, and the late-afternoon sun slanted in on them.

"Here," said Parrish, crunching over the leaves and taking George over to a blackened stump. It was hollow inside. "Thometimeth people take my thtuff. I hide thingth here. You can too if you want."

"Hey, man. Thanks." They set off back down the

slope, and Joelene, looking out, saw George taking Parrish home. Parrish took his hand as they walked out the driveway. Joelene, watching them, found another soft ache, this time in her throat, as George bent down and scooped up an armful of leaves and threw them over his friend.

At dinner that night George complained that he missed having television. He missed watching *Jeopardy!*

"OK," said Joelene, slipping a third slice of pizza onto her son's plate. "Pretend I'm Alex Trebek. 'American Literature for three hundred dollars. *Gone With the Wind* was her only book.' "

"Who was Margaret Mitchell?" said George.

"Right. 'Foods for one hundred dollars. A chorizo is one of these.' "

"What is a sausage? Mom, don't keep playing this. I'm going out for some air." Joelene went to say something but changed her mind. Trust, she thought.

"Don't be long. I'm going to sit with Uncle Percy and put his papers into some kind of order."

Outside, George went to the garage and unpadlocked the door. He opened one side gingerly, hoping it wouldn't squeak, and slipped inside. He bolted the door behind him and felt above his head for the string to pull on the light bulb. Then he opened the trunk of the Mustang and climbed inside. It was a bit of a squeeze because he was so tall, but he wriggled himself into position and pulled at the back partition that separated the trunk from the main body of the car. He had found a fingerhold last night when that crazy dude had shoved him in and taken off like a bat out of hell. At first George had only been searching for a handhold to steady himself as they careened around corners and bumped over sidewalks. But then he had been surprised when the partition, crumbling like everything else in his mother's car, gave way and he could put his whole hand into the upholstery of the back seat.

That's when he had discovered the money. At least, it felt like money. It smelled like money too. There were bundles of it. He had shoved the partition back into place as he felt the car coming to a stop. "Out," the dude had said, and hauled him out by his jacket. George thought he was going to be shot. But the dude said, "Get lost, fast," and George had taken off along the highway, stumbling in the dark, expecting to hear a bullet ping into his back at any moment.

George wasn't sure if the money would still be there. He yanked at the partition, and it came off and he threw it behind him and groped inside. The money was there. He pulled out two thick wads and twisted around to hold them up to the light. One was a bundle of twenties, the other of hundreds. They were not all new notes, some were old and crumpled, but they were stacked face up and held by rubber bands. George whistled. He began pulling more and more packets out of the upholstery.

From the way they were jammed in, George thought they must have been packed from inside the car. Someone must have taken the seat off to do it. But who? It was a fluke that he had found it. George had never seen so much money.

"George? Are you in there?"

Joelene's voice made his heart stop. He began stuffing the money back where he found it. "Yes, Mom."

"George, what are you doing? Parrish phoned. He left his hat here. Will you let me in?" George was sweating. He thrust the last wads into the space, jammed the partition into place, and scrambled out of the car. He grabbed a length of coiled rope from the newly cleared workbench, unbolted the door, and then saw that the trunk of the car had sprung open. A bundle of money that he had missed was in clear view. George jumped to the car and sat on it, and the trunk clicked shut as Joelene pulled open the door.

"We ought to oil this," she said. "Are you smoking?"

"Mom, don't you trust me?"

Joelene sniffed suspiciously. "What are you up to?"

George stood up. "I just thought I'd get this length of rope. Didn't Pete say something about taking me out on fire drills? I want to do some climbing."

"Climbing."

"Here's Parrish's hat," he said, picking up the red-peaked cap from a stack of chairs. "I may as well return it to him now. I'll just jog it over."

"Jog."

"Yeah. I'm getting fit, Mom. This is the new me." George backed out of the garage with the rope slung over his shoulder and the cap in his hand. "Jogging. Exercise. Weight lifting. Climbing." He went through motions of upper-arm curls and deep knee bends. Joelene followed him out and he quickly padlocked the doors and took off at a slow jog, his sandals flapping. She watched him suspiciously as he turned around under the street lamp and gave her a victory salute with his arms raised as though he were Rocky Balboa.

Joelene walked slowly back to the front door. It was a mild night, and she stood for a moment silhouetted against the light on the front steps, savoring the moon. There were two clipped yew hedges on either side of the front porch. At least they had once been clipped; now they were ragged and spread with—Joelene picked at the fluff on one—hair, human hair. Uncle Percy got it from the barbershop and insisted it kept the deer from eating the hedges in the winter. Joelene rubbed her fingers together with distaste and went inside. She did not see a small movement across the street, where a man hunched in a blue Lakers jacket shifted his position and settled down to wait a little longer.

Joelene was having a dream. She dreamed she was outside and it was dark and the night air was like Jell-O. It cleaved around her as she crashed and fractured her way through it. Every fracture made the sound of chalk dragged on a blackboard. She was trying to walk with her arms tight beside her and her breath held to see if it made any difference, when a small sound woke her. At first she did not remember where she was until the cold night air coming in the open window told her she was in Uncle Percy's house. She sat up in bed with a start. She had not left the window open.

There was a muffled sound in the dark, a movement she could sense but couldn't see, and then a hard hand clamped itself across her mouth.

"One word, lady, and you're dead."

He squeezed her jaw so tight she thought it would break. She felt something cold and sharp against her throat.

"The keys," he said. "I want the keys to the car."

The hand came away slowly from her mouth and the sharp thing at her neck pushed in harder. "There," Joelene said. "Over there," but no sound came out.

"Come on," said the man. "I ain't got all night. Where're the goddam keys?" He made a vicious little move with the knife and in doing so tripped over the hard hat that Joelene had beside the bed. "She-e-it," he cursed. For a split second he released the pressure on Joelene's neck and she screamed and it didn't sound at all like her. There was a crash as the door flung open and the light went on. The light was blinding. The man spun around; he was wearing a nylon stocking over his head. George stood naked in the doorway except for his white boxer shorts. He let out a cry like Tarzan and lunged for the ax on the floor, and the man saw him do so and turned and ran for the window. In the same split second as George threw the ax like a tomahawk, the man somersaulted through the window. The ax crashed through the upper pane and landed with a thud on the wooden veranda floor. There was a yelp of pain. George rushed to the window and climbed through and lunged after the man, but he sprinted down the street and into the darkness before George reached the front gate. He hobbled back to his mother and climbed in the window. There was blood on one bare foot.

"Got a glass splinter. Are you OK, Mom?"

Joelene was still sitting up in bed, looking shocked and holding the sheet up to her chin. Across the hall Uncle Percy was banging his walking sticks up and down, demanding to know what was happening and calling for his rifle. Joelene couldn't get her lips and teeth to work. George ran to the kitchen and brought back the leather and silver flask from her pocketbook. Joelene took a sip and then took a deep breath and her wits came back to her.

"Are you OK, Mom?" George rubbed her hand. Joelene nodded. Her voice squeaked and then she tried again.

"Why does he want the car?" she said. "Who is he?"

George sat on the bed and extracted a sliver of glass from his heel. "I don't know."

Uncle Percy hollered from his bedroom. "Joelene!"

Joelene got up and put on her wrap and went to see Uncle Percy. She turned around at the door. "It's only an old Mustang."

"I'll go and put on some hot chocolate," said George.

"And ring the police," said Joelene. "He put a knife to my throat."

"Tell you what," said George. "I'll ring Pete. He'll know what to do."

Joelene thought of all the questions to be answered again. She was scared but she was tired. "Oh, let's wait till morning, then," she said. "I'll sleep in your room. He won't come back tonight."

"Right," said George. "First, though, I'll just check everything's OK outside. Back in a minute." He was out the window before Joelene could call him back to put on a robe and a pair of shoes. Joelene pulled her own wrap tighter, took a deep breath, and went in to calm down Uncle Percy.

Five

Thank you for using AT and T."

"Hello, boss? It's me."

"Yeah, yeah, yeah, I know it's you. You're the only guy who calls me collect. What do you want? Did you get the car?"

"Boss, I'm in trouble."

"Did you get the car, Ernie?"

"I tried to hot-wire it. I couldn't get it to start. Had to take the door off the garage to get to it, too. Got a padlock as big as a—"

"What happened, Ernie?"

"I woke Joelene up to ask her for the keys."

"Shit. Did she recognize you?"

"What do you think? I wore a stocking. My own mother wouldn't have recognized me."

"Ernie, did you get the keys?"

"That's the problem. Her son heard me . . ."

"George."

". . . and he threw an ax at me. It went through the window. I went through the window. Jeez. I thought he was going to scalp me."

"Ernie. I want that car. She took my friggin' money! You know what I'm saying? I got bosses too, right? They want their cash. They want it now. They make neckties with our tongues. You know what I mean, Ernie? 'Ooh, I'm sorry,' I'll say. 'I'm late with your money. My girlfriend took it with her to New York and my stupid friggin' sidekick can't get it back.' You think they're gonna believe me? Get it, Ernie. Today! And don't call me collect anymore!"

"Hey, boss, there's one more thing. I broke my arm going through the window. But it's OK; I got Blue Cross. Hello? Hello?"

The next morning the police came and asked all the usual questions and left Joelene with a telephone number to call if she needed them. When they had gone Joelene admitted that she was feeling very nervous about being in the house alone. So Pete and my dad drew up a roster of all the local men to keep an eye on Uncle Percy's house. Pete boarded over the broken window until the new glass could be fitted and Moira took Joelene to the doctor, who checked the small cut on her throat and gave her a tetanus shot. The garage door was lifted back onto its hinges, and everyone puzzled over the Mustang and why anyone would want it so bad. Pete crawled under it and kicked the tires but could offer no explanation. George watched nervously.

"Have you any idea, Joelene, why anyone would want it?"

Joelene shook her head. "It's beyond me. It belonged to Tom so I kept it for sentimental reasons. I've spent more money fixing it than it's worth." She looked over the car as if she was saying goodbye to it and said, "I think I might sell it."

"Oh, don't sell it, Mom. I love this car." George leaned over the hood and hugged it protectively.

"Well, don't you worry about a thing," said Pete, taking his leave of her. "If I'm not here, Buddy or Pool will be. No one will get in again."

"Thanks. I appreciate it."

Pete hesitated. "If you like—uh, if you want to take a break for an hour, maybe tonight we could grab a bite to eat at the diner."

"Oh, but Uncle Percy—"

"There'll be someone here. We've got the old two-way working too—if he needs you, they'll just call us and you can be back here in eight minutes."

"Well"—Joelene made up her mind—"that would be fine. I'd like that."

"Seven o'clock?"

"Seven o'clock."

° ° °

Late that afternoon, a UPS truck delivered a box to Joelene.

"Why, it's from that nice shop in the mall," said Joelene, taking the box into the kitchen and showing it to Uncle Percy. Uncle Percy was lining a pair of shoes with newspaper, cutting out shapes of the soles from the *New York Post.* Joelene slit open the box and pulled aside some tissue paper.

"Why, mercy," she said. She held up a short, bright red plush coat. It had one big button and shoulders like a linebacker. There was a card. *"From an admirer,"* she read. She giggled and slipped it on.

"What do you think, Uncle Percy? Does it suit me?"

Uncle Percy looked up and grunted. "Waste of money," he said. He slipped another piece of newspaper into the sole of his shoe.

Joelene dashed into the hall to have a look at herself. "It must be from Pete," she said. She came back in. "Or Moira?" Uncle Percy looked up at her from under his eyebrows. "No, not Moira. Then who? It's so lovely and warm. Feel it, Uncle Percy." But Uncle Percy wouldn't be cajoled and sat with his scissors ready to start on another page.

"Oh, save that," said Joelene, glancing over his shoulder and picking up a page he was just about to cut. " 'How to stop flannelette sheets from pilling in the dryer.' Now that's a hint we could use in this house."

Uncle Percy made a gargling sound and swore. But nothing could shift Joelene from her sunny mood. She refused to think about the weirdness over the car and the fright she had had last night. The red coat revived her. She hugged it to her, humming. The color was wonderful—warm, alive, vibrant. It made her feel as if she were in California again.

"Why, hello, Joelene, Pete," said Gerry at Chuck's Tastee Diner as they sat down in a booth. She handed them a big shiny menu card. "I'll be right back. We are so busy tonight."

Joelene slipped off her coat and placed it on the bench beside her.

"Great coat," said Pete. "Is it new?"

Joelene looked at him from under her eyelashes. "As a matter of fact, yes."

"Suits you," said Pete. Joelene waited for him to go on, but he said nothing.

"I thought—" she began, and stopped. "Nothing." She looked around the room. The diner was packed with locals and transients.

"Seventh-Day Adventists," said Gerry, coming back with two big glasses of water and plonking them down on the pink laminated table. She was wearing a pink corsage pinned to her lapel. "They had a meeting tonight."

"That's pretty," said Joelene, touching the corsage.

"Thank you," said Gerry, and then, leaning forward, whispered conspiratorially, "George gave it to me, but don't tell Mike." She stood erect. "What'll it be? Tonight's specials are"—she flicked over her little notebook—"charred chicken and blackened catfish." She giggled. "That's the way Chuck always cooks. Now it's fashionable."

"I'd just like a salad and a burger," said Joelene.

"Bibbendivearugulaoricebox?"

"Bibb."

"ThousandIslandFrenchItalianorhousedressing?"

"French."

"Raremediumorwelldone?"

"Medium."

"Frenchcottageorbakedpotatoes?"

"You choose."

"The cottage fries are great."

"Cottage."

After Pete had been through the same process and Gerry had rushed off in her short little candy-striped dress on her flashing brown legs, Mike Astanazy, released from his dishwashing chores for a five-minute break, came over and stood at their table. His hand was soft and puckered from the hot water as Joelene shook it. He had deep dark eyes and long curly black hair, held back tonight by a pink busboy's hat.

"You on for the midnight shift?" asked Pete. "At Percy's place?"

"I hate to put you to all this trouble," said Joelene.

Pete's chest expanded. "It's nothing."

"Be glad to do it," said Mike.

Gerry came back with their orders balanced precariously on her two thin arms. Mike looked at her adoringly. She rushed off again.

"I don't plan to be doing this forever, Mrs. Mathieson," said Mike. "My mother wanted me to make something of myself. I'm hoping to get into the police force. I got one more test."

"That's nice, Mike. I hope you make it."

"What I wanted to say is I been practicing my observation powers, like. And there's this guy. I've seen him here a few times. Making eyes at Gerry. Tried to make a date. All over her like sauce. She told the bum where to get off." Mike cracked his soft-skinned fingers one by one as he spoke, and Joelene thought of George's long skinny neck under Mike's thumbs. "Tough-looking little guy. Always using the phone booth. Wears a Lakers jacket. Yeah, an out-of-towner, but we get a lot of those here. But he was all jumpy when youse—excuse me, *you* two came in. He's been hiding out in the john. I seen him go in there and he hasn't come out. Got his arm in a cast."

A bellow came from a guy looking at them through the kitchen hatch.

"That's Chuck," said Mike. "I got to go. I'll be around later, Mrs. Mathieson. Don't you worry about a thing."

"I better check this out," said Pete, wiping the last of his burger from his mustache and standing up.

"Do you think you should?" said Joelene. "What if he's violent? Shouldn't you get some help?"

"He's probably just passing through. Mike's made mistakes before. He and his motorcycle buddies once trailed a car he thought was carrying illegal weapons."

"And was it?"

"Yep."

"And was the driver arrested?"

"Nope. It was the police chief. Under cover."

"Oh."

Pete strolled to the john and went in. There were two stalls and only one was empty. Pete knocked on the closed door.

"Say, mister. Can I have a word with you when you're finished?"

There was a clatter from inside and the sound of glass breaking, and Pete put his shoulder to the door of the stall and heaved. It didn't give way, but he heard a muffled oath, a grunt, a scrambling noise. He pushed again, and the door sprung open just in time for him to see a leg disappearing through a high square window. There were footprints on the seat.

"Hell," said Pete and ran back for his two-way radio and his hat. He grabbed Joelene's hand as he went by. "He went out the back way." Joelene grabbed her coat, and they tore out of the diner and through the parking lot. Mike came running out behind them, tearing off his apron.

A car shot forward from an alley and they got out of its way just in time. No sooner had they caught their breath than the car was reversing toward them. "Out of the way!" screamed Pete. He pushed Joelene to the side, and they rolled on the gravel as the car sped off. Then Pete was on his feet, pulling Joelene up and running for his pickup. Mike had reached his motorcycle, and it roared into action.

"This is Firefly to Red Rooster," said Pete into the two-way as he screeched out of the parking lot, did a U-turn on the feed road, and shot up the fire lane onto the freeway. "Tell Smokey to give me backup. I have Foxy with me and Brando on wheels. Chasing Noah's perpetrator in a black Chevrolet sports coupé. No number."

"Foxy?" said Joelene. Pete allowed himself a grin but didn't take his eyes off the stream of traffic ahead.

"There he is," he said, gunning his pickup forward and squeezing between two slower vehicles. The cars honked like mad. Pete could read the registration number now, and he called it in.

A warning sign flashed by that they were approaching the tollbooths. The road began to widen out into the plaza. Behind them came the wail of sirens. The driver of the black Chevy must have heard them too because he suddenly swung from the fast lane to the middle lane and back to the fast lane and spun his car 180 degrees and shot off in the direction in which he had come.

Pete swung the steering wheel of his pickup too but he was too late; the tollbooths reared up in front of him and he applied the brakes and they came to a shuddering stop sideways to the tollbooth and inches from impact. The police cars and Mike's motorbike piled in behind them. There was a terrible screech of metal as the two police cars collided and Mike's bike catapulted him ten feet into the air. He landed with a thud and for a moment lay there before he sat up, shaking his head, still in its lifesaving helmet.

The toll taker ran out to him, and Mike gazed up at him with a smile. "Oh, hello, Mr. Morgan," he said as my dad reached him. "How you doin'?" And then he passed out.

Six

Next afternoon Pete took George out to the gravel pits where the volunteers were practicing fire drills.

George didn't want to go. It was a miserable day, and the wind blowing straight down from Canada was raw and biting. The house was so cold he had gone back to bed and climbed under his Navaho blanket, which still held grains of sand from past picnics at Malibu. George was miserable. He was homesick. Why, he told himself with horror, he was even missing Vanna White, and he hated that show. George plugged in his earphones and sulked.

Joelene came in. There is nothing that makes a parent more mad than the sight of a teenager in bed after midday. Joelene was no exception.

"George Mathieson! Up! Out!" She pulled off his blanket.

"Oh, Mom. It's threatening to snow in the boonies! They said so on the forecast."

"You won't melt. Pete's here. You said you wanted to go on a fire drill."

George groaned.

"You were going to get fit. Jog. All that stuff. Now get up and go to work on your pectorals."

George gave up arguing and went to work on his pectorals.

Under the guidance of the fire chief, the volunteers had set up the shell of an old abandoned car in the gravel pit and doused it with gasoline. At a signal they lit it, and it went up like a torch. The wind quickly fanned the flames into a furnace. Pete and Buddy and Pool first went through a make-believe rescue, smashing in the windows of the car and heaving a dummy out through the window. Then they all took turns running the hoses out and playing them on the burning wreck. The fire chief timed them with a stopwatch. George tried to help, but he kept getting in the way.

Pete was a big man but without the gut that some of the other men carried. He was strong. George went to help him with a coiled section of the hose and found he could hardly lift it. Pete laughed as he watched him struggle and then went over and lifted it with ease. "It takes a bit of practice," he said.

George and he were about the same height, but George's shoulders were half the width. George watched him as he wiped his blackened hands and face on a rag from the engine. There was a fresh burn mark on his cheek.

Pete grinned at him. "What are you thinking?"

"Why do you do this? You could get hurt."

Pete swung up onto the fire engine beside the ladders, and George clambered up beside him. He squeezed his knees sideways so he could get in. The other men climbed aboard and they set off for town. It was almost dark now and freezing cold, but George felt warm after the exercise.

Pete shrugged. "There are a lot of old wooden houses around here. Winter's coming. Ever seen a real blaze and heard a kid screaming at a window? It's not a pretty sight."

He slapped his hand on George's knee.

"I hear you're interested in climbing—want to try it tomorrow or the next day? We could get in an hour after work tomorrow before it gets too dark."

George was lackluster. He just wanted to get home. "Sure," he said, with no enthusiasm.

"I'll bring some music. Ever hear an original tape of the Dead concert with the Quicksilver Messenger Service . . ."

George pivoted and nearly bounced off the fire engine. " 'Scuse me?"

". . . at the Fillmore Auditorium in San Francisco?"

"You have a tape?"

"I was there. I used to go to all their concerts, when

I could afford a ticket or a plane fare. Jerry Garcia was my hero. Man, what he could do with that guitar. And Bob Weir on the rhythm guitar?" Pete whistled. "You should have seen Pig-Pen on the organ."

"What do you think of Carlos Santana, then?"

"The Latino guitar player? He's phenomenal. I'll bring my guitar over one night and we can play to their tunes."

"Electric?"

"Acoustic."

George saw Pete in a whole new light.

They reached the firehouse and jumped down. George helped wash down the fire engine and stow things away. He found he liked the easy camaraderie of the group. There was a lot of joshing around, which made the work go quickly.

"So, tomorrow, then?" said Pete when they had finished and everyone was going home.

"Sure," said George. "Great, man. Hey, you're a cool dude."

Pete laughed, but all George could see were his white teeth gleaming. Pete jammed on his Stetson.

"Pick you up after five," he shouted, as he let the clutch out on his pickup and took off. George walked home singing the words of "Dire Wolf" at the top of his lungs. "Don't murder me, plee-ease, don't murder me."

o o o

On the other side of town, Ernie was munching down aspirins with a glass of milk. His arm hurt. His ulcer was playing up. He had to get wheels. He had dumped the black Chevy as being too recognizable. He had to find another car rental place, not easy out here in the boondocks. Until then he had to figure out how he was going to get about. What he needed was an inconspicuous vehicle, something everyone took for granted. Meanwhile, he'd lie low; give everyone a day or two to relax their guard. Yeah, that would work. It would also give his boss time to cool off. Besides, he thought, spilling another aspirin into his hand, he didn't feel so hot.

"Where's my chain saw, woman?"

It was a few days later, and Joelene was washing down the walls in the hallway. Under the years of grime the walls turned out to be a soft yellow color. A low warm sun shone through the panes on either side of the door. Joelene turned her head. Uncle Percy was standing rigid in his doorway.

"What are you doing out of bed?" Joelene came down the ladder and dropped her sponge into a bucket.

"Lies! Lies!" he shouted. "You're stealing from me. You don't really care 'bout me. Where's my things? I can't find any goddam thing. Where're my bankbooks?" He began rattling his walker up and down.

Joelene peeled off her rubber gloves and walked past

him into his bedroom. She picked up a blue cardboard file folder and pulled out the little books. "They're here," she said, handing them to him. "Under 'B' for 'bankbooks.' He took them from her, trembling. "As for your chain saw, George says he saw it out on the porch where you'd used it to cut a frozen meat loaf in half. I'm not taking anything from you, Uncle Percy," she said softly. "I'm beholden to you for giving me and George a home."

"No one does nothin' for nothin'," he said. He licked his finger and began turning the pages. Uncle Percy seemed to be shrinking. The skin on his neck that used to wobble like a turkey's was now stretched like the skin on a roasted drumstick.

"It's all there, Uncle Percy."

He licked his finger again and turned another page. "You been readin' this stuff? Stickin' your nose in again where it's not wanted?"

"If you tell me to leave, I'll leave. It's just that George seems to be making friends here. He's out now with Pete and Parrish, fixing the door of the ark."

Uncle Percy looked up over his eyeglasses. "Did they go inside?"

"No, they know better than that by now."

Uncle Percy hawked deep in his throat. "Did they fix my winder too?"

"All puttied in. George did it. He's turning out to be quite handy."

Uncle Percy turned and made his way to the front door, opened it, and spat.

"I've got things I have to do, woman."

"Joele-e-ene," said Joelene, putting out her hand for the bankbooks.

Uncle Percy trembled. "Where's my chain saw, then?

Joelene laughed. "What're you going to do with a chain saw, cut down a tree?"

"I've always cut my own wood," he said with dignity. "I can still lift that saw if someone helps me."

"I'll get Pete and George to cut some."

"Pete." Uncle Percy spat out the word. Joelene looked at him.

"OK. I'll ask George to go with you." Rebellion sparked in Uncle Percy's eyes. "No George, no chain saw." Uncle Percy nodded.

"At least it'll get me out of this goddam house for a few hours. Don't feel like my house anymore."

Joelene folded her arms like a tradesman and surveyed her handiwork. "Don't you like it? I thought it looked a nice happy shade of yellow."

"Looks like eggs to me," said Uncle Percy. "I hate eggs."

A few hours later, Uncle Percy was sitting between George and Parrish as George drove up the old lumber road behind his house. George was driving the truck.

George knew the road. Pete had brought him up here to a rock face he used for what he called basic climbing. George's arms still ached from pulling himself up that cliff. "Relax," Pete had said. "Learn to trust the rope. You're wasting energy. Climbing," he'd said, "is a mental thing." George straightened out one of his long arms with a wince.

The soft surface of the road had been chopped and churned by other trucks and motorbikes. Mike Astanazy and his friends used it all the time. Mike had been kept in the hospital for twenty-four hours for observation, but he was fine now. The whole town was buzzing with his exploits. Even Gerry had told George she couldn't date while Mike was feeling so poorly. Poorly, my ass, thought George. He had seen them at the movie theater, and Mike was doing just fine, particularly when Gerry kissed him and all.

Uncle Percy had put on his wood-cutting trousers. They were beige and tough as denim, frayed and holey and oil-stained, and if you shook the cuffs, sawdust fell out in a stream. He wore a plaid wool shirt, a blue cap with a long peak and *Giants* written on it, and an old shrunken cardigan of a no-longer distinguishable color, the back of which rose up in a big wave below his shoulders.

"Over there." Uncle Percy waved and they turned off and bounced along a secondary road to a clearing. A large white pine lay on its side.

"That's it," said Uncle Percy. George backed up as close as he could. "I've been cutting this tree for years."

George and Parrish helped Uncle Percy out of the truck.

"Get your hands off me," Uncle Percy said to Parrish. Parrish sighed and shrugged and let go. George and Uncle Percy hobbled over to the tree. The tree had many branches showing cuts, but the main trunk had not been touched. "Prop me up over there," said Uncle Percy. He pointed to an angle of a huge branch where there was already a small pile of neatly cut logs on the ground. "I didn't have the strength to pick them up last time."

Uncle Percy shook his head as he thought how weak he had become. He had always been a strong man. In the days when he and his brothers ran the family lumber company, he had got out and swung an ax with the best of them. But now the company was long gone, his brothers were both dead, and his time was coming too. Uncle Percy gritted his jaw and thought about something else.

Once he was in place, jammed between the trunk and his walker, George hefted up the chain saw for him. It was a beauty—powerful, shiny, well-oiled, and sharpened. Uncle Percy carefully checked the fuel mixture, motioned to George to screw the cap back on, and then, with a smile of great glee, pulled the cord.

The chain saw roared into life. Uncle Percy adjusted the throttle and with the most delicate precision placed the rotating teeth on the nearest branch. Soon a whole row of neat lengths lay like a sectioned worm on the ground. George put his Walkman back in his ears and sank into the Grateful Dead. Whenever Uncle Percy nudged him, he shuffled the walker a few more inches or angled the chain saw so the weight was carried by the tree trunk. Parrish had brought along a scout knife and spent his time whittling at fragments, or—giggling—carving his initials inside a heart, or just happily throwing the knife into a tree trunk as though he were skimming pebbles in a stream.

The sun, which had been sporadic all day, came out in the late afternoon and threw long shadows and brilliant light around them. Small beads of sweat had broken out on Uncle Percy's face. There was only one mishap when Uncle Percy, forgetting his lack of strength, swung the chain saw down as he used to in the old days and the teeth bit into the walker's aluminum frame with a metallic screech and stopped. Uncle Percy looked up, surprised, at George, and George laughed with relief. Uncle Percy laughed too. At least George thought that he laughed.

"Time to quit anyway," said Uncle Percy. He was quivering with fatigue and excitement.

George had lit up a joint. He was wearing his sandals as usual, and there was sawdust all over his socks. He was shaking his feet to loosen it.

"I'll try one of those," said Uncle Percy, sitting on the trunk and admiring his work.

George hesitated and then offered him a joint. Uncle Percy put it to his mouth and looked puzzled.

"Why do you want this stuff?"

George shrugged and his earring twinkled. He answered it like a *Jeopardy!* quiz. "What is pleasure?"

"Hmmph." Uncle Percy examined his gnarled hands. There were little cuts and calluses all over them.

"Why do you do this stuff?" said George, indicating the chain saw and the tree and the logs with a toss of his head.

Uncle Percy looked at him. "Because it lets me know I'm alive. If I cut myself and I bleed, I'll know I'm not dead yet."

"Your heart's weak. It will kill you."

Uncle Percy looked at the stub between George's fingers. "What's it to you? At least I'll know I've lived."

George got up, and he and Parrish began collecting the logs and throwing them in the back of the truck.

"Ever had a job?" shouted Uncle Percy across the clearing.

"Nope."

"Gives a man a purpose."

"Yeah. A chain around his neck. Man, I don't need much. I'm getting by fine."

"Living off your mother."

"Don't give me that. I help her."

"A man needs a purpose. Help me up."

In the truck, jostling down the road again, Uncle

Percy raised an earpiece from George's ear. "I said, did your mother ever tell you about me? About your grandfather?"

"What's there to tell?" asked George, taking off his headphones.

"Nothin'," said Uncle Percy, examining the headpiece. "I wanted to be an engineer once. Wanted to build things."

"Is that what that contraption in the back yard means? Has it got some kind of solar power system?"

But Uncle Percy wasn't listening to George. He had put on the headphones. The set was too big for his small, delicate head, and the wires stood up like a halo. But it was the expression on his face that made George laugh as the pounding beat of Jerry Garcia thumped into Uncle Percy's cranium at a rate of decibels and clarity that Uncle Percy had never imagined.

"Hey, man," said George to Parrish. "Check out this dude."

"All right!" said Parrish, clapping his hands.

George squeezed Uncle Percy on the shoulder. "Yo! There ain't nothing wrong with *your* head, man."

George dropped Parrish off at his house, where a forlorn group of fellow tenants hovered in the yard. Roy Harper, who looks after them, was standing with them. Roy is a tiny, bald man who is always cheerful.

"What happened?" said Parrish, jumping out of the truck. "I thought you were all going to the movieth."

"We were, but someone stole our van," said Roy Harper. He chortled.

"Firtht the Muthtang, now thith," said Parrish. "I bet the thame guy took it."

"Why would anyone want a rust-bucket like our community van? It doesn't make sense." Roy Harper stopped laughing, which for him signifies great distress. "I'll have to let Health Services know," he said. Everyone looked gloomy. The health service people are always coming out to the home and getting on everyone's backs.

George turned to Uncle Percy. "Uncle Percy, mind if we drop these folks at the movie house? It'll only take ten minutes."

"Where'll they all fit?"

"We don't mind sitting in the back."

"Well, I dunno," said Uncle Percy.

"Hop on," said George. "Let's ride." So everyone climbed into the truck bed, including Roy Harper, and settled themselves on top of the wood, and George drove them to the mall, where the Starlite Movie Theater complex was showing six movies, three of them starring Clint Eastwood. Uncle Percy didn't speak until he and George were alone again.

"Gas costs me a dollar nineteen a gallon."

"I know what gas costs."

"I cain't go gallivanting across the county whenever I feel like it."

"Then I'll pay you, OK?"

"You ain't got any money."

George kept his mouth shut tight for a minute and then said, "I can pay you. And another thing, I don't need a ticket to California from you anymore."

Uncle Percy's head squeezed down onto his neck. "Oh? You come into some money, George?"

"I'm not saying. Just that I don't need it anymore."

A flash went across Uncle Percy's face as they passed under a street lamp and turned into their driveway.

"You ain't been thievin' from me, George, have you?"

"No, I ain't been thievin' from you, Uncle Percy. What have you got to steal?" George laughed as he yanked on the hand brake. He waved to Lars, standing across the street.

But Uncle Percy was really worried. He stared at George. "My bankbooks, my bankbooks." He could hardly get out of the truck quick enough. George helped him but he shrugged him away and scuttled into the house with his walker. George followed him, laughing softly, and stood at the door of his room as Uncle Percy's fingers scrambled through his folder. George shook his head.

"You don't trust anyone, do you?"

"You get to my age, son, you'll find there ain't no one you can trust. No one."

"I hope not," said George softly, as he watched Uncle

Percy find his books, lick his finger, and go through the pages, one by one.

"What's that?"

"I just said I'll still help you if you want me to. But the deal's off. I'm not doing it for money."

"Then whatcha doin' it for?" Uncle Percy had found that the small balance in his bankbooks remained unchanged. He snapped them shut and twisted his lips in a grimace of relief.

"If you have to ask, you wouldn't understand," said George.

"Fool," said Uncle Percy. He reached for his pills beside the bed. "Fools and women, that's all I'm surrounded with."

Uncle Percy clapped his pills into his mouth and gulped a glass of water. Then he straightened up and looked at George as though he hadn't seen him before.

"You *have* taken something, I know it." His eyes began searching his room. "Now what is it?" He began pulling at the bedclothes, lifting the blankets. He rattled a walking stick through the papers on the dressing table. He turned in a circle in the middle of the room. George left him mumbling to himself and searching distractedly through his things.

In the middle of the night Uncle Percy remembered what was missing. He stood over George's bed like an avenging angel and shook him. George had no idea how he'd got into the room so quietly.

"I jist remembered. It took me all night to work out what you took. My rifle. Where's my goddam rifle?" said Uncle Percy.

"Shhh. You'll wake Mom. I forgot about the rifle. It's in her room. I hid it that night."

"You sold it."

"No, I didn't. Look, I'll go and get it, OK? Then we can all get some sleep." George tiptoed out of bed, through to his mother's room. He walked carefully to avoid the pitfalls on the floor. The gun was still hammocked in the lace cover. He hooked it out, holding his breath. Joelene turned in her sleep and he froze for a moment. Then he lifted the gun free and tiptoed back to his own bed. Uncle Percy took the rifle from him lovingly. He ran his hands over the stock, opened the breech, and checked. It was empty.

"I took them out," said George.

"Cain't shoot a gun without bullets."

"Can we go to bed now?"

Uncle Percy sighed. "I cain't sleep."

George ran his fingers through his hair. "Neither can I, now." He pulled on a robe over his shorts. "I think I'll get something to eat. You want something?"

"No, but I'll come along."

In the kitchen George cooked a frozen French bread pizza in the toaster oven.

"What you need here is a microwave oven," he said.

"I heard about them ovens. Fella at the hardware

store says he puts hardened glue pots in his and in ten seconds he's got liquid."

"Yeah. You can use them for cooking, too."

Uncle Percy found there was still some brandy in Joelene's flask and asked George to add hot water to it.

"This must have cost plenty," he said, holding the silver and leather flask in his hand.

"Yeah. It was a present from her boyfriend. He likes flashy things."

"You don't like him."

"There's nothing there to like."

"I never did understand women's taste in men," said Uncle Percy, sipping his drink at the kitchen table. "Women always mean trouble."

"Is that why you never married?"

"Never thought about it much. Thought about it once." Uncle Percy stopped talking and sipped his drink. "Terrible thing to get old," he said.

George bit into his pizza. "What was my grandfather like?"

Uncle Percy moved his glass around on the table. The overhead light threw all the bumps and angles on his head into relief. His cheekbones stood out like polished bone. "Norman."

He took another sip of brandy and water.

"He couldn't handle his liquor."

George pretended to be disinterested and started on another piece of pizza.

"Ah, what's the use? He was a no-hoper, spoiled rotten by our mother—I guess because he was a pretty baby, an easy birthing. I was ugly even then. Norman wore skirts till he was seven. She could never bring herself to cut his hair: long blond curls. One day Dad had enough and he pinned Norman down on the floor with his knees and took the scissors to him. That was the only time I ever saw Norman not get his own way. That and one other."

"What other?"

"I don't want to speak ill of the dead. Might be joining 'em soon."

"You didn't like him?"

"I hated him." Uncle Percy looked at George as though he was surprised by what he had just said, and George looked at Uncle Percy: at the thin, wrinkled skin now pulled taut on his skull with age and sickness, at the wide thin lips and the pale blue eyes, at the surprisingly slender bone structure of his hands underneath the nicks and calluses and hard skin and the concave nails that were ridged and split from woodworking. George looked back at Uncle Percy's eyes and saw a long, skinny tear had welled up and spilled unchecked down one cheek.

George said nothing. He had never seen a man cry. But he had seen his mother cry when his father died, so he recognized grief when he saw it. But then he couldn't work out why you would cry for someone you hated. He thought about it. They sat on quietly in the kitchen with no sound except the hum of the refrigerator going on and off and outside the occasional bark of a neighborhood dog. The kitchen clock gave erratic ticks as the minute hand stuck on its journey around the face.

After what seemed a long time, Uncle Percy rose to his feet. "I think I'll go to bed now."

George watched him go to the door, where he paused and turned.

"You help me tomorrow, George. I'm runnin' out of time."

Seven

George stood wearing a leather apron at a table in the bowels of the ark. He held in his hands a piece of wood shaped like the soundboard of a violin, except it was two feet long.

"Kinda purty, ain't it?" said Uncle Percy. He was sitting with his legs akimbo, his hands on one of his walking sticks and his chin resting on his hands. "We need eighteen more of them. Going to use them as struts."

"Struts for what?"

"For the stalls. Mangers. Now come over here." Uncle Percy's chair was fastened to a small platform with swivel casters for feet. He had made it himself to get about more easily. He spun along the length of the table. Behind the table on a series of shelves was an array of beautiful tools. There were smoothing planes and tiny thumb planes and hole-boring tools and brace bits and carpenters' squares and sliding bevels. There were different kinds of saws: a tenon saw, a dovetail saw, a hacksaw for cutting metal. There were spirit levels, and a chalk line and reel, and chisels and gauges, and everything was in order, not disorder like Uncle Percy's house, where it seemed as though everything had defeated him.

"You've used a jigsaw before, right?" said Uncle Percy. "You hold this end. This one here's the template. Watch me." Uncle Percy switched on the power and guided the wood under the saw. It was done in no time and he started another, and then George took over. He soon got the hang of it after a few false starts, at which Uncle Percy cursed and called him a dullard. But Uncle Percy was a changed man inside the ark. Gone was the cynical and suspicious expression on his face. Instead it seemed his brow had opened up. George glanced at him once or twice as he changed over the pieces.

Uncle Percy was in his element as he worked now with a chisel and hammer, now with emery paper, smoothing out splinters and roughness till the curves were like glass. Here in the ark the world to Uncle Percy was no longer impenetrable but absorbed and understood. There was no part of the ark, no plank or furbelow, no nail or hasp, not even a described space between the decks, nor shapes of air caught in the ropes of the staircase, that Uncle Percy did not love. This was his world, a world he had created and which represented that tender part of himself he had hidden for so long. Now it was revealed like the flesh of a mango when the skin is bent back.

When they had a number of struts ready, Uncle Percy directed George to place them on the floor of a makeshift elevator. The toolbox was placed there too, and a large, powerful drill with a long orange extension cord snaked out behind them.

"And throw on that climbing gear," said Uncle Percy. George shrugged and did as he was told and threw on his ropes and harness and a few carabiners that Pete had loaned him. He had stopped asking Uncle Percy questions because he seldom got a straight answer.

"Now we go up," said Uncle Percy and pressed a button. George lurched for balance. There were no walls on the tiny platform, only a flimsy wooden rail.

As they soared up to the third deck and the counterweight passed them, George let out an involuntary gasp. The elevator jolted to a stop and Uncle Percy rolled himself out, using his feet to propel him.

"What do you think?" he asked. George didn't know what to think at first. The deck at this level had become a gallery that encircled two thirds of the ark. In the middle the ark was open to the sky. The floors of the decks were polished wood, the planks pegged together with wooden dowels. And ranked all around the walls were open stalls, horse stalls, each one separated from the next by a curved partition and each entrance flanked by a pair of braided wooden columns, some mahogany, some fruitwood, some oak, some cherry, each topped with a different finial depicting an animal. George touched a small erect wooden rabbit with awe.

"You made all this yourself, Uncle Percy?"

But Uncle Percy had moved out of earshot. He was gazing up at an enormous wooden portcullis that hung suspended by heavy chains above a closed drawbridge.

" 'And the animals came in two by two,' " said George.

"Damn thing stuck," Uncle Percy was saying. "I was trying to get it down last time when I got tangled in the goddam rope and nearly broke my neck. Shinny up there, George, and take a look."

George looked at his great-uncle with incredulity. "*Shinny* up there?"

"You afraid of heights like your mother?"

"No, but . . ."

"It's a piece of cake. I'd do it myself if I could."

"I could be killed, Uncle Percy."

"You said you'd help me. You want to practice climbing, here's your chance. Get up there."

George took off his earring. "Give this to Parrish if anything happens to me." Uncle Percy growled and George went over and tried to work out the best path up to the top of the portcullis. There was a beam he thought he could use to throw his ropes over. He sized it up as he slipped into his harness and tied on the rope.

"OK," he said. "I think I can get up and stand on that thing protruding there—"

"The corbel."

"Right, and then throw the rope across the beam, and then I'll work out what to do next."

Uncle Percy let out a cackle and George looked at him openmouthed. Uncle Percy was laughing. Uncle Percy couldn't stop.

"If you could jist see your face," said Uncle Percy, wiping his hand across his nose.

Weird sense of humor, George said to himself as he went to the wall and found himself a fingerhold. The first part of the ascent was not as bad as he thought because the edges of the planking gave him enough toeholds and fingerholds to keep inching upward. He thought he might put a rope on it one day and use it as a practice wall. Pete had loaned him an *étrier* he could use, something like a short rope ladder. Now he concentrated on the path he had to take.

He began moving in a crablike fashion, one step up, one step sideways. The muscles of his legs and arms were burning as he reached the projection that jutted out from the beam above him. A few more inches and he had made it. He eased himself onto the corbel, which Uncle Percy had carved into the shape of a cod's mouth. He attached a rope to his harness with a figure-eight knot. Then he braced himself and threw the other end of the rope out and over the beam. He missed, and the rope fell heavily to the deck below. He coiled the rope up again and tried a second and a third time. On the third attempt the rope caught and spun around the beam, and he grabbed the end and pulled it tight. Now George was able to belay himself across to the beam, and he straddled it and sat up on it, sweating and pleased. He signaled down to Uncle Percy.

Uncle Percy was twenty-five feet down. A few feet behind him the deck stopped and fell away sixty feet to the floor below.

"Can you see where the chain is caught?" shouted up Uncle Percy.

George examined the situation. The drawbridge was raised and lowered by an endless chain wound around three different-sized pulleys, rather like a bicycle gear, but the portcullis system was different. Chains attached to the top of the portcullis were eased over a series of blocks or wheels before they reached the other side of the hull, where a counterweight held them taut. The chains of the two systems had become entangled. The only way to disentangle them was to release the weight. And the only way for George to reach the weight was to cross a beam that vaulted over the void in the middle of the ark.

"Why'd you put the weight over there, Uncle Percy?" shouted George.

"Because I didn't know any better. I'm a carpenter, not an engineer. Can you fix it?"

George carefully judged the alternate ways of getting to the counterweight. But he had no choice. He tried to remember everything Pete had taught him. He blew out a deep breath and relaxed his diaphragm. The beam was just wide enough to crawl on, though it looked a damn sight more narrow up here than it did to Uncle Percy. He decided to use some small pitons and a rope, knowing that his need was more psychological than physical.

He lay on his belly and set out, tamping in his pitons as he went, snapping on the carabiners and threading through the rope. He didn't look down until he reached the other side, and the rest of the crawl was a breeze. He was at the last pulley wheel now and could see that the counterweight was made up of a large block of metal with a number of added sandbags. Uncle Percy pressed and released the power, but nothing happened.

"I need some slack!" shouted George. He made his way down and sat on the metal counterweight, got out his knife, and cut the rope that suspended one sandbag. The block he was on jolted up a few inches and nearly threw him off. The sandbag crashed to the bottom of the hull and split open with a thud. The portcullis remained stuck fast.

"It's not goin' to work," shouted Uncle Percy. "Come back!"

George shinnied along the beam, more confident now with the rope in place, and crabbed his way down to Uncle Percy.

"There's another way," said Uncle Percy. "But we'll

have to rig the chain up to the other system and use that to take the load. I have to think about it." He took off his cap and scratched his head.

"Uncle Percy, you really going to fill this thing with animals?" asked George as he stepped out of his harness.

Uncle Percy put his cap back on. "What do you think, George? Where am I goin' to find a giraffe around here?"

George laughed. "Or an elephant."

"Or a rhinoceros." Uncle Percy pushed himself toward the toolbox. "No more games. We got work to do. Then I've got to go to the hardware store."

"Uh, Uncle Percy, we can't go to the hardware store until Mom gets back from Moira's."

"I've got my own truck."

"She distinctly said, 'Don't let Uncle Percy go to the hardware store.' "

"I don't care what she said. I'm not a prisoner. I need things to fix that there mechanism, damn bugger."

"We'll have to wait."

But Uncle Percy wasn't listening. He took one of the carved pieces and scooted over to the nearest stall carrying the electric drill in his lap. The rest of George's words were lost under the whine of the drill as he screwed the strut into place.

° ° °

"Excuthe me, George, where'th Uncle Perthy going?"

George shot off of bed at the sound of Parrish's voice. He had left Uncle Percy resting in his own room and had lain down himself and must have fallen asleep.

"Isn't he in his room?"

Parrish followed him into the hallway, where George saw through the open door that Uncle Percy was not in bed.

"He took the truck," said Parrish. He turned his head so George could look at his profile and pointed to his ear. "He gave me thith. Thaid you gave it to me."

George's diamanté earring dangled by a string from Parrish's left ear. George grinned.

"It's yours. Doesn't go with my new image." They went outside. The weather was still mild, although there was an undercurrent of cold air in the wind that made George zip up his windbreaker. The last few leaves on the maple trees along the street were rustling as the breeze picked up.

"Which way did he go?" said George, looking up and down the street.

"That way." Parrish pointed.

"Where's the nearest hardware store?"

"That'th got to be Gimlock'th in the mall."

"Near the movie theaters? Parrish, can I borrow a bike?"

After George left, pedaling furiously on an old ten-speed, Parrish took up his usual post on his porch. He took off the earring, which he had hooked over his ear, and examined it again with delight. "I'll have to get my ear pierthed," he said. He hooked the earring back on and waited. Soon enough he saw Joelene driving by in her orange Mustang.

Joelene hadn't wanted to take the car out, but Uncle Percy needed his prescription filled. Surely, she thought, the car would be safe enough to leave in front of the drugstore for a few minutes. So she had taken the risk and now she was driving home with relief.

"They're not home," said Parrish, when he caught up with her. He talked to her through the open driver's window. A leaf blew in and caught in her hair. Joelene looked cold. The glass had fallen down into the door and she could not wind it up.

"Uncle Perthy went off in the truck and George went after him on a bike."

Joelene groaned. "Do you know where they've gone? Hop in."

Parrish gave directions with a great grin on his face.

Driving past the empty showground on the way to the mall, they passed a man pasting up a billboard advertising a circus. Parrish hung his head out of the window, holding on to his peaked cap until it was out of sight. He sat back in with his hands folded on his lap.

"My brother joined the thircuth," he said.

"What does he do?"

Parrish shrugged. "He travelth a lot."

Joelene glanced at him. "Parrish, is that George's earring you're wearing?"

Parrish looked apprehensive, as though he thought she would take it away from him. "George gave it to me."

Joelene smiled at him. "I think it's very nice."

George reached the hardware store and parked the bike. The hardware store at the mall was more like a supermarket and sold everything from cordless telephones to slug repellent. Gimlock's motto was, "If we ain't got it, you don't need it."

Outside, stacked against the wall, were sacks of road salt and a battalion of snowblowers. In summer these were replaced by bags of peat moss and lawn mowers. There were six cashiers in a row, all busy with people buying starter cables and humidifiers and flatware and Rubbermaid garbage cans. George couldn't see Uncle Percy. He went up to a big black woman who had just finished with a customer.

"I'm looking for a little old man with no hair using two walking sticks."

"Does he wear a Giants cap with a big frayed peak?"

"Yeah, that's him."

"And a pair of ol' trousers that leaks sawdust all over the floor?"

"Yeah, that's him. Is he here?"

"No, I ain't seen him today. Hey, Linda," she said, "can you help this guy?"

"I'm looking for a little old man with no hair using two walking sticks. Have you seen him?"

"Oh, you mean Uncle Percy."

"Yeah, Uncle Percy."

"Try aisle twelve." George set off from the checkout.

"He's *always* in aisle twelve," the black woman shouted after him.

George found Uncle Percy standing mesmerized in the middle of aisle twelve, leaning on his walking sticks. He had a supermarket cart with him, and he was looking at rows of small plastic trays containing brads and wood screws and nails and washers and hex nuts and toggle bolts.

"I could do with a few of these," he said, glancing up at George as he loomed up beside him. "Count me out twenty, and don't forget to screw a washer on each one. Damn fools try to cheat me. Wrong sizes sometimes."

"Uncle Percy, aren't you ashamed of yourself?" said George, ripping off a bag from a stand and filling it with bolts.

Uncle Percy looked at him. "Nope." He turned his attention to a whole other display, of hinges and spring door closers and tile nippers and strapping tape. He picked things up and handled them and marveled at their ingenuity or workmanship. There was a whole box of assorted white plastic couplers and tubing glides that stopped him in his tracks and he examined them minutely, turning them over and running his thumb against the edges. He kept asking George to fill up another bag, and soon there were nine such bags in the cart.

"I'm gettin' tired," he said. "But I sure could do with a mastic gun. And we need some lighter-gauge chain. And handles. We need handles, George." George could see that Uncle Percy's movements were slowing down. Each tiny shuffle was an effort for him.

"Wait right here," said George. He ran across an aisle and picked up two bags of foam rubber pieces and pushed them into the cart to form a seat. Then he picked up Uncle Percy before he could protest and sat him in it. Uncle Percy writhed.

"Damn bugger you are, George. Let me out of here! Let me out!" He waved his sticks and hollered but he didn't have the strength to get out and George sped along the aisle with him, pushing him like a baby in a perambulator. Uncle Percy started to laugh. He looked like a crazed little gnome. They whizzed up to the end of aisle twelve and George did a wheelie with the cart and let his feet slide, and then they spun around and went off across the store.

"You're goin' the wrong way," shouted Uncle Percy. "Aisle eleven, aisle eleven, that's where they keep the chain."

"Whoops," said George, sliding to a stop and preparing for another spin.

"George, is that you?" George spied Joelene along the aisle. She was right beside a rack of cedar closet fresheners cut in the shape of teddy bears.

"They're on to us," said George. "Hang on to your hat." He gave the cart an almighty shove and then jumped on himself, and he and Uncle Percy zoomed across the back of the supermarket. George could see Joelene in flashes as she ran along a parallel aisle.

"George Mathieson, you stop this minute!"

George gave a last devilish kick with his foot on the floor and readied himself for a spin, but suddenly he had run out of aisle. A towering display of kitchen canisters and tin trays and cookie jars and sink mats and do-it-yourself wine racks began to topple as they hit it. It seemed to teeter and stop as George and Uncle Percy looked up at it above them. Then it all came crashing down as they covered their heads. George took his arms down too soon, and a net bag of medicine balls bounced off his head and down the aisle.

"Are you OK, Uncle Percy?" said Joelene, running up to him, followed by the floor manager.

"Of course I'm OK," said Uncle Percy, with as much dignity as he could muster. He pulled a blown-up pink bath pillow in the shape of a shell out of his lap and dropped it on the floor.

"Oh, it's you, Uncle Percy," said the floor manager. "I might have known."

"It's my fault," said George. "I got carried away."

"Have you two finished your shopping?" said Joelene, beginning to pick up some boxes.

"Leave it, leave it," said the floor manager. "I don't want any more things broken."

"No, I ain't finished," said Uncle Percy. "I need chain and I need handles, and I expect a discount. You overcharged me last time. Yes, you did, don't deny it. I knew your father and your grandfather Gimlock when he was a boy. We went fishin' together. He wouldn't charge me what you folks do for things that break before you even get them into place. Ball cocks that don't float. Masonry bits that wouldn't drill butter."

"Uncle Percy," said Joelene, "you're making a scene."

Uncle Percy whacked the side of the cart with a walking stick.

"Am I goin' to get some attention here, or"—he stared at the hapless floor manager—"do I have to speak to your mother?"

The manager sighed. "I'll get someone to cut you a length of chain, Uncle Percy. Just let's move on so we can get this place cleaned up."

A few minutes later, as they were toting up things at the checkout counter, Parrish came rushing in waving his arms.

"He thtole it," he shouted. "He thtole the car again!"

"Who stole it?" said Joelene, as they rushed out of the store into the parking lot.

"The man in the Lakers jacket. I wath thitting there lithening to the radio and he jumped in and threw me out." Parrish started to cry. "I lotht my earring."

At the curbside where Joelene had left Parrish sitting in the Mustang with the engine running there was now an empty space. Behind it sat the missing community minibus.

George whistled. "I just thought of something I have to do. I'll follow you back on the bike. Uncle Percy, you go with Mom and don't get into any more trouble." He helped them into the truck with their purchases. Parrish dawdled beside the recovered van.

"Can you drive this thing?" said George.

"Of courth," said Parrish, who had never driven in his life. He got in and started the engine. The engine stalled. Parrish got out with a swagger.

"I think I'll call Roy," he said and sauntered off to the phone booth.

George was just getting on the bike when Uncle Percy's truck passed him. He looked up and saw Uncle Percy mouthing something at him through the window.

"What?"

Uncle Percy wound down his window and bellowed out, as Joelene drove off, "They forgot my discount. Ten percent. Damn buggers."

Eight

I'm sorry, Mr. Ernie, there is no reply at that number."

"But there's got to be. There's got to be."

"I'll try once more."

"Oh, jeez, boss. You better be in a good mood."

"I'm sorry. Still no answer."

"She-e-it."

"Thank you for using AT and T."

Saturday, I remember, was a red-letter day because Uncle Percy had agreed to take a shower. Joelene had rescued a tubular aluminum chair from the garage and placed it squarely in the shower stall. Uncle Percy had forbidden her to buy one.

"No women," said Uncle Percy, as he left his room.

George made a thumbs-up sign and winked as he followed Uncle Percy to the bathroom. He was carrying his tape player.

"Shower-washing music," said George as he shut and locked the door.

I was in the kitchen with my mother and Joelene. Everyone tended to congregate in the kitchen in Uncle Percy's house, which was funny considering that Joelene didn't cook. There was a living room, but it was so full of Uncle Percy's things that there was no place for anyone to sit.

Moira and Gerry were carving jack-o'-lanterns to decorate the firehouse because Wednesday was Halloween. A bowl of colored gourds sat on the table.

"I haven't done this for years," said Joelene, who was making a costume for Pauline. Pauline wanted to go as a prom queen. She's into all that kind of stuff. It's all Gerry's influence. Joelene was taking up the hem of an old evening dress that belonged to my mother. My mother would have sewn it, but Joelene was sticking it up with tape and a hot iron. "Somehow Halloween goes with the seasons on the East Coast," Joelene went on. "Pumpkins and orange leaves and frost in the morning. It's not the same when you just throw a cape over your bikini."

Moira looked up and laughed. It had been a long time since she had worn a bikini.

"Last year," I said, "Jack Miller went as a condom."

"And he didn't win any prizes," said Moira, scooping out some pumpkin flesh and banging it into a pot. Pauline brought in some big branches from the garden and began wiring artificial leaves onto them.

There was a fresh gust of music from the bathroom as the door opened and shut and George appeared in the kitchen with a sheet and a towel and said, "Stage Two," and cleared a space near the back door and put down the sheet and placed a chair on it. Then he went off and came back with Uncle Percy.

Uncle Percy was pink and glowing. He had on a clean plaid shirt and a pair of trousers rolled over at the waist because he had lost so much weight. He looked kind of pleased with himself. "Make some coffee," he said to me as George sat him on the chair. I got down the old grinder from the shelf, put some beans in it, placed it between my knees, and started grinding.

George spread the towel with a flourish around Uncle Percy's shoulders and pinned it together with one of Joelene's pink hair clips. I saw he had a bowl with him and scissors and a razor and a shaving brush. We all looked at him, astonished.

"Just carry on," said George, "and ignore us." He began working up a lather with the brush and soap. Uncle Percy sat meek as a lamb with his eyes shut, and when George started applying the foam he turned his head this way and that and offered his old stubbly chin to the razor and never complained once.

"What are you going as?" said Joelene to me.

"Dan Quayle," I said.

"Your father won't like it," said Moira. "Just because you want to be a journalist one day, dear, doesn't mean you have to go around upsetting people now."

"I think it's silly," said Geraldine, picking up another pumpkin.

"Oh, does Mikey vote Republican, too?" I said.

"He seems a sensible young man," said Joelene soothingly.

"How's his head?" I asked.

"It's fine, thank you," said Gerry, with a warning glance at me, "but his bike's a write-off."

"Yeah, I saw him down at the bike shop yesterday," said George, giving a final trim to Uncle Percy's remaining wisps of hair. He handed Uncle Percy a hand mirror from his mother's pocketbook. Uncle Percy examined his face as though he were looking at a stranger; he looked pleased but noncommittal. And then he put the mirror on his knees and looked at each of us. His eyes didn't waver. It was a weird feeling.

"You look terrific," said Moira. "You did a good job, George."

Geraldine got up, holding a whole goop of seeds in her hand, and went over and stretched up on her tiptoes and kissed George on the forehead. "I think you are very sweet," she said. Women are so fickle.

Geraldine spread the seeds in an oven pan and George

began to clear up and I poured some fresh coffee and then Parrish came in from the hallway.

"A big red Merthedeth with California plateth ith coming up the thtreet," he said. It was the longest sentence I had ever heard him say.

Uncle Percy's euphoria ended abruptly. "More damn kin visitin'," he said.

"No," said George, putting a hand on his shoulder, "not kin. It's my mother's boyfriend."

"Don? Here?" Cousin Joelene suddenly went all nervous and pretty and checked her image in the mirror Uncle Percy had put down. I couldn't work out if she was pleased or frightened. A little bit of both, I decided. As she went to the door I whispered to my mother, "Is this *the* Don Diamond she keeps talking about?"

"Ssshhh."

We were all listening like mad as Joelene opened the front door, but all we could hear was the Grateful Dead wailing in the background.

"Well, guess who's here?" said Joelene, coming back into the kitchen and clapping her hands.

"I can guess," said George.

She said in an angry whisper, "George, I want you to behave, you hear? I don't want any trouble."

George looked across Uncle Percy's head. "If he lays a finger on you, I'll kill him."

"Don," said Joelene loudly, "come in and meet my oldest living relative." A big man came out of the hallway. Poor Pete doesn't have a chance, I thought, looking at him. Don Diamond was in his forties, dapper in gray slacks and a yellow shirt with a brown leather jacket on the top. His gray hair was full as though he brushed it back with a blow dryer, and he wore a gold pinky ring on his left hand. He came forward to shake hands with Uncle Percy, stepping carefully on the sheet to avoid the hair. I noticed he wore shoes with tassels. And he squeezed carefully past the pumpkins with his hand across the flat of his stomach, or thereabouts, so he didn't get any pumpkin goop on him.

"I don't want to interrupt a family gathering," said Don, turning on about one hundred and fifty watts of charm all at once. His pointy teeth, fully capped, were all showing. Uncle Percy's lips withdrew from his own teeth in a grimace that was close to a snarl. We were all introduced, and that's when I noticed that Don Diamond's eyes were as pointy as his teeth. His teeth were like those of a wolf, white and gleaming and sharp, and his eyes had the same kind of expression, like an animal's, dazzling and cunning, with all his wits carried on the points of the canines. This was some bad dude, as George would say. George turned away so he could avoid his handshake and Don said with a laugh, "Still got no manners. You ought to teach that boy of yours a thing or two, Joelene."

"How long are you staying, Mr. Diamond?" said Moira, as though he were the kind of man you normally meet in a kitchen in Poughkeepsie. Moira is a certified cardholder of the Miss Manners School of Etiquette.

"Well, that depends on Joelene," said Don. He slipped an arm around her waist. "She left kind of sudden."

"And you drove all the way from California to see her?" said Moira.

"That's about it," said Don. "We got things to talk about."

"We must be going," said Moira, flicking her eyes at me and my sisters.

"Oh, you don't have to go," said Joelene, escaping from Don's grasp. Don took a monogrammed handkerchief out of his pocket and passed it across his big nose.

"I don't think I can carve another pumpkin," said Moira. "It was so nice to meet you, Mr. Diamond."

"Likewise," he said.

"I'll catch up with you later, Mom," I said. "I'll ride my bike home."

Moira and my sisters left and I busied myself with another pumpkin and Parrish opened a can of soup.

"I'm tuckered out," said Uncle Percy, without glancing at anyone. "George, help me to my room. Goin' to listen more to them Dead Ends of yours."

When George came back into the kitchen, he opened the refrigerator to get out a can of Coke.

"So how long *are* you staying?" he asked Don.

"For as long as it takes."

"Takes to do what?"

Don had sat down and crossed one well-shod foot across the other. Even his socks were monogrammed. It was as though he couldn't remember who he was unless he kept reminding himself.

"How long it takes to persuade her to come for a little holiday with me."

"Oh, I don't think so, Don," said Joelene.

Don stood up and shook out his trouser creases. He was a restless man, and he paced up and down the kitchen looking at everything and filing it away for future use. He stretched his neck inside his collar, shot his cuffs, squared his tie knot. Everything about his clothes was flawless. I could see George wanted to throw a can of Coke over him and show him in his true colors.

"Joelene," said Don, coming to a rest near the back door. He had lowered his voice, and it came out smooth as caramel. "Joelene," he said. "You got something of mine, babe." He suddenly remembered we were still there, though I was trying to make myself invisible. He must have seen my eyeglasses glint or something. "Do these kids and that idiot have to stay in here?" Parrish and I backed out fast, though I would have kicked Don Diamond in the butt if I had more courage.

George said, "I won't leave, and don't talk about my friend that way."

"Please, George, I can handle it," said Joelene. George left the room reluctantly and came and leaned against the wall of the hall with us. I edged closer to the kitchen while the guys went into a huddle near the front door.

"Joelene," said Don. I watched him as he put his arms around her.

"Don't, Don. Why are you here? Did you really drive all the way from California?"

"I missed you."

"Really?"

"Honest. Missed you around the office." He kissed her fingertips. "We had that little row"—he kissed the inside of her wrist; he had to push up the sleeve of her white sweater to do it—"and you just took off. No message, nothing. Missed everything about you." By now he had snuggled his head down between her ear and her shoulder. Joelene's arms were still hanging down. He squeezed her shoulders up in an embrace and then kissed her fiercely. I've never seen Dad kiss Moira that way.

"Don, don't." But her arms had come up.

"I even missed seeing that old car of yours parked in the yard. Remember I kept telling you to park it in the back because I thought it was bad for business?"

"Oh, Don," said Joelene, suddenly withdrawing from him, "my car's been stolen."

"Stolen?"

"Yes. This is the third time since we got here. I can't understand it. No one can."

"You sure it's gone?"

"What do you mean, am I sure? Of course, I'm sure. Some little guy stole it from the mall yesterday."

"You saw who it was?"

"No, but Parrish did."

"Oh, the mongoloid. What does he know?"

Don Diamond is the kind of guy who would kick a dog if he thought no one was looking. Joelene cuffed him, but it was very halfhearted, and then Don kissed her again with his eyes open and he saw me over her shoulder and came over and shut the door.

"What does your mother see in him?" I said to George.

"Beats me. I asked her once, and she told me to mind my own business."

"Probably animal magnetism."

"What'th that?" said Parrish.

"Sex."

"Ondine, you think everything is caused by sex."

"So did Freud."

Out of the kitchen came Don and Joelene.

"See you at seven, then," he said. He ignored us as he went out. It had begun to snow softly, and he sort of ran for his car.

"You're not seriously going out with him?" said George.

"How could I say no, George? He drove all the way here from California to see me. I forgot to ask him if he sent me that red coat."

"Mom, think. How can you be so naïve?"

"Excuse me, George, I don't need you to talk to me like that. I know what I'm doing."

Joelene walked back into the kitchen and turned on the oven. George followed and took hold of his mother's arm. "No, you don't, Mom. You just hate saying no to people. You know he's bad. You know he's trouble."

Joelene took a tray of pumpkin seeds and sprinkled salt all over them like Moira had told her to. "Then why *did* he come? Do you know, George?"

George hesitated. Joelene slid the tray into the oven and banged the door shut.

"George, if you're keeping something to yourself, something I should know, you should tell me."

"It's just that—Jesus, Mom. He's in the mob or something. You can smell it on him. That car showroom was just a front. He laundered money for the Colombians. I saw some of his receipts. Don't you remember those funny-looking guys who would keep appearing at the showroom?"

"You've been watching too many movies, George. They were customers. I never saw anything wrong when I worked for Don."

"Because you're blind, Mom. You don't see what you don't want to see. It was the same with Dad. You believed he was going to make the big time and you kept seeing that house you always wanted and dreaming about it and talking about it and buying seed catalogs and planning the yard and—gee, Mom, you thought one day it would really be yours. But it was *never* going to happen. We're never going to have a house like that. I'm never going to be on *Jeopardy!,* Mom."

"What's got into you, George? Haven't I taught you to always look on the bright side of things?"

"You have to face reality, Mom."

"All I've done is say I would have dinner with Don tonight. He's staying at the motel on the Thruway. Now I don't want to hear any more about it, I have a heap of things to do."

George came out of the kitchen and slammed the door so that the whole house shook. He looked at the telephone. "I'm going to call Pete," he said.

Ernie was hanging around the reception area of the Blue Vista Motel when he saw Don Diamond's car turn into the forecourt.

Ernie whimpered, "Say it isn't so," and dived into the telephone booth. He had no sooner folded the door closed and sat down cradling his broken arm when Don saw him and crashed back the door and grabbed him by the collar. Ernie winced as Don hauled him out of the booth.

"Hello, boss," said Ernie brightly. "What are you doin' here?"

"I could ask the same about you, you twerp."

Don lifted Ernie so that his feet were no longer touching the floor and frog-marched him out of the glass doors into the corridor that led to the rooms. Then he pinned Ernie against the wall, holding him up by the collar.

"What do you think you're doing, Ernie, eh?" Don stiffened the fingers of his other hand and shoved them into Ernie's chest. The back of Ernie's head hit the wall. "I send you from California to do a simple job." *Shove.* "I says, 'Ernie, since it was your bright idea to hide the friggin' money in the car in the first place, you can go and get it back.' But you can't do it. You got one dame, one boy, an' an old man to deal with, and you screw up. And you know something, Ernie? You got me scared. Because I got guys out there asking me questions. They're asking me questions I can't answer, like when am I going to pay them what I owe them. You know what I mean?"

"Sure, boss."

"No, you don't. They're calling me at home at night, breathin' down the phone. I don't like that. They blew up a car, Ernie, one of my goddam Porsches at the showroom. That was a message, see? So I'm scared, Ernie. I can't even get to the airport 'cause they're following me. So I drive here. I drive all this friggin' way to this dump." *Shove, shove, shove.* "Because you can't deliver my money."

Ernie whimpered. "Jeez, I'm sorry, boss."

"Where's the goddam car? Or should I break your other arm?"

"I got it hidden in a barn a mile from here. But boss, you gotta know this, I tried to tell you; the money's gone."

The pronged fingers hit Ernie's chest again. "How can it be gone, you asshole?"

"I swear to God, boss. I tore the seat out. I ripped out the upholstery. There's nothing there. The money's gone."

Don let go the hold he had on Ernie's collar, and Ernie slid down the wall and sat on the floor.

"Bitch," said Don. He shot his cuffs, stretched his neck, and squared his tie. He put one polished toe into Ernie's side and kicked. "Get up," he said. "Go get my luggage out of the car. I got a date tonight, and I don't want to be late."

George and Uncle Percy had set up a workshop in the glassed-in veranda off the kitchen. Uncle Percy was sitting on one of the chrome kitchen chairs with his legs apart, his head down, and his hands busy as usual. George took satisfaction from the gleam that bounced off Uncle Percy's shining head. His baby-pink skull positively shone through the wisps of silky hair.

"I'm so damn clean I don't feel like myself anymore," said Uncle Percy, as if he knew what George was thinking. He sat with a sheet of newspaper on the floor between his feet, and on it lay the inner parts of a radio.

Not a modern plastic transistor like George had, but an original old radio with a fabric insert on the wooden face and round knobs and a needle that pointed to the stations.

"That must be fifty years old," said George. Uncle Percy had him whittling another finial for the ark. It was supposed to be an alligator perched on its hind legs.

"I reckon," said Uncle Percy, pausing with a spring in his hand to cough to one side. Snow sifted down outside and closed them into their own little world. George got up to put the light on. He could hear his mother humming to herself in the kitchen.

"Uncle Percy," he said. "Suppose you knew something about someone who was real bad and you had a way of getting at them that would really hurt, what would you do?"

Uncle Percy coiled the spring delicately with his scarred fingers. "Like learn 'em a lesson?"

"Yeah."

"I'd learn 'em."

George went back to his whittling. "It sure doesn't look like an alligator." He held up the piece of pinewood he had been working on.

"Looks more like a pineapple," said Uncle Percy, screwing the back onto the radio.

"That's it," said George. "I'll make it a pineapple." He began scoring into the soft wood of the belly with his knife.

"You still hankerin' for California?"

"Yeah. A bit. No, come to think of it, it's not California I miss, it's things. Like television."

Uncle Percy placed the radio on a table beside him, and George put down his work and plugged the radio in. Uncle Percy turned the radio on, and the dial glowed green. He twirled the knobs slowly and faint music crackled over the air.

"I never did want to leave Poe-kipsie," he said. "Oh, once, when I was young and rebellious, I told my old man I wanted to go to sea. Kept talkin' about it. Drove him crazy. He said he needed me here for the lumber business. Never did go. Came to my senses."

"I wish Mom would come to *her* senses. What is it about women, Uncle Percy, that makes them so . . ." For once George was at a loss for words. "So irritating?"

"I been trying to figure that out all my life, boy."

George whittled away at his alligator/pineapple for a minute. Small chips of wood fell to the floor like nail parings.

"Would you teach me how to shoot the rifle?" said George, without looking up.

"I reckon I could. Used to like a bit of target shooting myself once." Uncle Percy put out his hand for the carving. "Cain't watch you torturing that thing for one more minute. Go and get the rifle. You'll find a red box of cartridges right beside it."

George brought back the rifle, tiptoeing through the

kitchen when his mother's back was turned. The rifle was wadded up in an old oil-stained sweater, along with a cleaning rod and gun oil. He unwrapped it, and Uncle Percy showed him how to clean the barrel. George watched how Uncle Percy handled the rifle, all his movements slow and deliberate, precise as a marksman. He watched how he felt the weight of the wooden stock, the pleasure with which he hefted the rifle in his two hands, the slow ease with which he raised the sight to his eye.

"Used to be good at this," said Uncle Percy. "Light's bad now. Tomorrow you can set up a target behind the ark. Ain't no one in the woods back there, 'cept sometimes that damn fool friend of yours, Parrish. Cain't turn around without him poppin' up somewhere. What's he do back there? Gives me the heebie-jeebies."

"He doesn't mean any harm. He's like a little kid. He says some of the other guys steal his stuff, so he hides it in a tree."

George examined the cartridges in the box as Uncle Percy went through the motions of loading and unloading. The bullets were like little brass candles with a dab of lead on the projectile end. The shell itself was brass, and the end was copper.

"Purty, ain't they? Wouldn't think one of those could kill a man, would you? Get the feel of it," said Uncle Percy.

George lifted the rifle to his shoulder and cocked his head to see through the sight. He looked along the length of the veranda to the far window and saw Parrish's head bobbing in the hairline.

"Get in here, Parrish," he shouted, without removing his eye from the bead. He saw Parrish grin and then disappear.

"What you got to remember, boy, is don't hold your breath. You just breathe in and out; don't anticipate the recoil. And when you shoot, always shoot a little lower to compensate for the bullet rise."

George lowered the rifle and wrapped it away in the sweater. It was dark outside, now. Tomorrow morning he would set up a target and practice.

Parrish came in the back door looking sheepish with his tongue between his lips.

"Hi, Uncle Perthy," he said. "Don't you look clean!" Uncle Percy growled. Parrish smiled at George like a child waiting for something to be noticed. "Look at my ear, George." Two shiny gold loops were inserted in the cartilage of his newly pierced left ear.

"Hey, you're changing, man," said George, laughing.

Parrish swaggered over to the table where lengths of copper wire and rolls of tape lay scattered in among year-old newspapers. He rummaged around for some matches, found them, and lit a cigarette that dangled from his lips.

"Grath," he said, inhaling and smiling at George and Uncle Percy. "You want one?"

"Christ," said George, glancing at the kitchen door

and going over to Parrish. "You can't smoke that here, my mother will kill us." He snatched the joint from Parrish's lips, and Parrish's mouth trembled. Joelene came to the door just then. George held the joint behind his back.

"Hello, Parrish. I didn't know you were here." Joelene gave Uncle Percy a glass of water and watched him swallow his pills. She was holding a paper wrapping in her hand. "I'm going to change and get ready to go out. George, dinner's in the microwave. I don't know what we ever did without it."

"Wish we knew who sent it," said Uncle Percy, with a glance at George.

"Uncle Percy, will you try and eat just a little tonight?" said Joelene.

"What's for dinner?"

Joelene read off the paper wrapping. "Chicken and rice with almonds."

"I'll try." The three men smiled at her. Joelene paused. "You guys up to something?"

"Oh, just, you know, guy talk," said George.

"Mmmm." Joelene was suspicious.

The men waited. George's fingers behind his back were burning.

Joelene swung on her heel. "I won't be late. I'll be at the diner if you need me. Don't forget to wash the dishes, George."

"I won't Mom." George let out a deep breath and

dropped the burning butt on the floor and ground it out. "Parrish," he said, "you mustn't do everything I do. You'll get into trouble." He looked into his friend's eyes. "Do you understand me?"

"Cain't say one thing and do another," said Uncle Percy.

"Look who's talking," said George.

Uncle Percy got to his feet and slowly shuffled toward the back door.

"Where are you going?" said George. Uncle Percy picked up one of his walking sticks. "I just want to take another look at that pulley. I think I've got a way to take the weight off." He stepped outside and held the door open and glanced back at George over his shoulder. "Well, are you comin' or not?"

George sighed. "Parrish, get yourself a beer. I'll be back in half an hour—I hope."

"Besides, I hate chicken and rice," said Uncle Percy. "Invalid food. Ain't your mother ever heard of meat and potaters?"

"You wouldn't eat that either."

"No, I guess I wouldn't."

Nine

Don Diamond dressed carefully for his date that night. Ernie sat mournfully on a chair in Don's room watching him get ready. The television, which was bolted to the floor, was switched on and a soft porno movie on the pay channel ran soundlessly behind him. Don had a towel wrapped around his waist and was brushing his hair carefully in the mirror. Don loved his hair. He counted every hair that came out on his comb and had nightmares of waking up bald one morning. He splashed on some cologne, splashed on some more, and then came over to Ernie.

"How'm I lookin'?"

The top of a big appendectomy scar showed above his towel.

"Jeez, boss, you look great. Ain't no gal gonna resist you tonight." Ernie still felt sick. His ulcer was playing up.

Don made a lewd gesture with his finger under his towel and laughed.

"You've got to be right."

"Joelene's just going to whisper into your ear what she done with that money."

"Good-lookin' chick, she better. Otherwise she might not be so good-lookin' tomorrow morning." Don laughed and dropped his towel and slipped into a pair of tight black briefs. "Whatcha got to understand about women, Ernie, is you have to play them." He began buttoning up a striped Sea Island cotton shirt. "They're like trout, see? You got to tickle along the top of the water and make them come to you. Cast the fly too heavy and they disappear."

"I didn't know you fished, boss."

"I don't, I saw it on television. Anyway, what's that supposed to mean?" Don flicked his discarded trousers across the bed at Ernie, who caught them in midair. "You think I'm an ignoramus, eh? Just because my father was a greengrocer and I didn't go to Harvard?" He threw across his shirt and underwear. "Make yourself useful and get these cleaned, Ernie."

He slipped on fresh trousers, sucked in his belly, and did up his fly.

"I'll show you how you should have handled this. This will be for your own good. First, I try the gentle approach, see? Take her out for dinner, soften her up. Then I bring her back here."

"What if she don't want to come?"

"What do you mean, if she don't want to come? Joelene? Me?"

"Well, she ran away from you in California."

"The woman's in love with me." Don stuck his face into the mirror and brushed his hair again.

"Then how come she took your money?"

Don turned and threw his heavy hairbrush at Ernie. He ducked and it hit a bedside lamp, which didn't budge. It too was bolted down.

"Stop with your friggin' questions." He shrugged himself into his leather jacket. "I think she took it to make a point. Yeah, that's it. She *knew* the money was there. She took it to make sure I came after her." Don shook his head.

"Oh, boss."

"Whatcha say?"

"I said, 'Yo, boss.' Go for it."

"Yeah, all right, then. I'll be back by nine-thirty at the latest. Here." He took some bills from his wallet. "Get a bottle of champagne in and two glasses, women love that, and make yourself scarce. Are you sure the diner is the only place to eat around here? What a dump."

"You look very pretty tonight, Joelene," said Don as he drove toward Chuck's Diner. The roads were icy and snow was still falling softly. He risked a glance over at her. Joelene was wearing a tight black skirt, and a pink sweater with ribbons woven through it peeped out from under her red plush coat. She had on a pair of impossibly high heels and, the way she had her legs crossed, her black clad calf looked seductive.

"Why, thank you, Don."

"Love that red," he said. Something in his voice puzzled her.

"You didn't send it to me?"

"Wish I had. If you and me get together, babe, I'll buy you all the coats you want." Don slipped his hand over Joelene's knee and up her thigh.

"Why, there's Pete," said Joelene, as they stopped beside a Chevy pickup at the lights. She moved away from his hand and pressed the button to lower her window. "Hi, Pete." Don lowered his head to look past her and saw a man with a mustache wearing a Stetson. Joelene introduced them.

"We're having dinner at the diner."

"Me too," Pete said. "See you there." And then the lights changed and Don gunned his car forward so that his wheels spun.

"I see you made friends," he said. He put his hand back on her thigh, but she moved away again and he had to put both hands on the wheel.

"Pete's been a good friend," she said.

"What is he, a cowboy?"

Joelene laughed.

"You got the hots for him?"

Joelene blushed. "No," she said, and looked out the window. Don drummed his fingers on the steering wheel. Things were turning out different from what he had thought.

The pink neon sign of the diner gloomed at them through the snow and they turned into the parking lot. Pete's truck came right in behind them.

"What a coincidence," said Pete, hitching up his jeans as he came forward.

"Isn't it," said Joelene, as Don firmly took her elbow and started for the bright lights of the diner. Joelene tripped along over the white snow.

"Cozy," said Don, shaking off the snow as they went inside. "Hope this doesn't mark leather."

"Hello, Joelene," said Gerry as they sat at a booth in her section. Joelene introduced Don. Don saw that Pete had taken a stool at the counter. He made Joelene change places with him so he could keep an eye on Pete. He didn't want her comparing them.

Gerry gave them a menu.

"Let's see what they've got to eat in this crummy place," said Don.

Gerry gave a perfunctory wipe of the table and raised her eyebrow at Joelene. "I'll be right back," she said, "to take your orders."

Don watched her sashay over to Pete and lean on the

counter talking to him. Saucy little bint, he thought. He smiled at Joelene. "How about some wine, babe?"

All through dinner, Don tried to touch Joelene. He would push his knee between hers, drop his hand under the table, and let his fingers crawl up toward her thigh, and each time she would move away or Gerry would come over.

"Jeez," he said. "What is this? What's the matter with you? You never used to be like this, Joelene."

"I'm sorry, Don. I'm just not sure about you anymore. I thought we might be able to talk some things over."

"Talk about what things? I came here after you, didn't I? Isn't that enough?" He lowered his voice and slipped his hand down again. "Oh, honey, you know how I feel about you. You know what I want to do to you."

"More coffee?" said Gerry, smiling and pouring it into their cups.

Don straightened up. "Get lost," he said.

"You see, Don," said Joelene, after Gerry had left with a toss of her long hair, "I've had time to think during the past two weeks. About us: you and me and George."

"George." Don sank back against the banquette. If there was one thing he hated it was when dames started talking about their children.

"About the future. Perhaps it's not in California for me after all. Perhaps it's here."

Don watched Gerry chatting again to Pete. Pete had

taken off his hat, and now he was lighting up a cigarette.

". . . carpentry. And he's learned to love Uncle Percy. I have too. He's part of a family I'd forgotten I had."

Pete reached into his pocket and Don froze. He's reaching for a gun, thought Don. He's a cop! Beads of sweat popped out on his forehead. He had left his own piece back at the motel.

". . . George said. You know I've always dreamed of a pink house with bougainvillea and a fountain. I had thought you and me might one day . . ."

But Pete took out a two-way radio, not a gun, and began to speak into it. Don relaxed a little. He could still be a cop, though. He watched Pete put the radio away, and then a guy in a long white apron came out of the kitchen, wiping his hands, and went over to Pete. The guy in the apron turned his head and took a good long look at Don. Shit, thought Don, a rookie cop if ever I've seen one! All his antennae were now up. This was a put-up job! He could feel it. His hair prickled on the back of his neck, and a little trickle of sweat was running down from one temple. It was no coincidence that Pete was at the restaurant. Joelene had to be in on it too.

"Are you listening to me?" said Joelene.

"Sure, babe. What did you say?" He looked back at Joelene. She was such a pretty woman, he thought, her orange-painted lips clashing so hotly with her sweater. What a pity, he thought. He put his hand on her arm and squeezed it.

"I want to leave. Now. I got things I have to ask you."

"Why can't you ask me here?"

"Joelene, I can't ask you here." He squeezed her arm tighter, and his teeth clenched as he smiled at her. "Smile, Joelene, or else I'll break your arm, right here and now."

"Don?"

"Shut up!"

Joelene and he stood up together. Joelene had no choice. He threw some money on the table and held her close as they marched out. His hand was like a vise on her forearm.

"You're hurting me."

"Get in the car." He could sense Pete had come out of the diner behind them. He pushed Joelene in from the driver's side and got in beside her and locked the doors.

"Don, what are you doing?"

"What's your friggin' boyfriend doing?" Don started up his car and swung out of the lot. "Is he a cop?"

"He's an insurance salesman."

"Sure," said Don. In the rear-vision mirror he saw the lights on the top of Pete's truck switch on.

"Where's my money?" said Don. "Give it back and I won't hurt you." He was driving with one hand, still holding her arm with the other. He gave another twist to her arm.

"What money?"

He shouted at her. "Stop playing games, Joelene!" His earlier veneer of suaveness was completely gone. He was staring through the swirling snow and keeping his eye on the truck tailing him. Pete was driving along steadily behind him. Now Don picked up the headlight of an outrider, a motorbike, tailing him too. "Shit!" He increased his speed.

"I don't know what you're talking about," said Joelene. "What money?"

She was facing him, her face horrified and wide-eyed. Don let go her arm and punched her in the eye, and she fell sideways onto the seat.

"Fuck you!" he shouted. "The money that was hidden in your car. In the back seat. I need it. You took it, you damn bitch!"

Joelene was crying. "I don't know what you're talking about. Someone stole the car. Perhaps they took it."

"*I* took the goddam car," said Don. "The money's not there."

Joelene sat up sobbing and took out a tissue from her bag.

"Then I don't understand it. There's only been George and me. . . ." Her voice trailed away. Her hand stroked the soft red pile of her coat. Don's face looked grim. He believed Joelene. If there was one thing he prided himself on, it was knowing whether people were telling the truth or not. Joelene wasn't lying. She didn't know where the money was. Didn't know there had been any money in the car to begin with. That left only one other suspect—George. "Only George and me." He increased his speed, watching the lights behind him.

"Where are we?" he said. "Where's the nearest phone booth?"

Joelene tried to get her bearings. "At the mall."

"How do I get there? Quick!"

Joelene peered out through the snow. Tears blinded her eyes and her left eye was beginning to close.

"Here, I think. Turn right."

Don's voice had calmed down. "Here's what we're going to do. We're going to go to the mall and you're going to phone George and tell him to come and meet us. You got that?"

"George doesn't know anything about any money."

"We'll find out."

There were late-night shoppers still about, and the concourse to the mall was busy with cars. The traffic light turned to red as they reached it. Don glanced in his mirror and accelerated and turned into the concourse. Cars honked furiously at him as they swerved out of his way. He flung the Mercedes into the parking lot of the mall, sliding on the snow as he wrenched the wheel around. He had lost the others, but only for a few minutes. He pulled Joelene out of the car and ran with her over to the phone booths. They were in a darkened area to one side of the entrance. Joelene's eyes frantically searched for the lights of Pete's pickup.

"Get in." Don tried to shove her into the booth. Joelene struck at him with her handbag.

"No! I won't!" She screamed. Don grabbed her arms with one hand and clasped his other hand over her mouth. Joelene bit him. He cursed and managed to push her halfway into the booth, but Joelene struggled and stuck one leg out of the door.

Suddenly the lights of the truck illuminated them. Don glanced up, startled, and Joelene elbowed him in the stomach. It hardly hurt him, but he let go and ran for his car. Joelene fell to the ground. "I'll get you for this, Joelene," he screamed as he disappeared into the swirling snow.

Pete came running up to her and Mike roared up on his bike. Joelene sobbed in Pete's arms as he tenderly lifted her face.

"How could I have been such a fool?" she sobbed. But Pete couldn't make out her words through her snuffling.

"Shall I go after him?" shouted Mike over the roar of his bike. He still had his apron on.

"Let him go," said Pete, helping Joelene to her feet. "I know where he's staying."

"Jeez, boss, what happened?"

"Shut up and grab our things." Don threw his clothes and hair brushes and pomades and toiletries onto the bedspread, picked up the corners, and made a bundle of them.

"We're leavin'. We'll take your car."

"What about the Mercedes?"

Don pulled up his trouser leg and strapped a gun to his calf.

"We'll get it later when things quiet down."

They ran out the outer door.

"Where's the car?"

"Over there, the Nissan. Rented it yesterday."

"I'll drive."

Ernie fumbled with the keys. The snow was falling thickly now.

"Come on, come on, come on!" shouted Don. He kept glancing over his shoulder to see if the the truck was coming. "Shit!" A state trooper's car pulled slowly into the motel forecourt. Don and Ernie threw themselves into the car. Ernie began to whimper.

"Shut up," said Don. "Sit still."

The police car nosed into the parking area like a shark cruising. It drove slowly past the line of parked cars and came to a stop opposite the Mercedes. Don watched it in his side mirror. The police car continued along the line and then drove back into the forecourt.

"Nice and easy, now," said Don as he started the engine. They drove at a regular speed out of the motel grounds and onto the side road. The snow swirled in their headlights.

"Where we goin', boss, back to California?"

"Not yet. Not till I get my friggin' money back. Stuck

here in this friggin' weather. No, we're gonna go to that barn where you've stashed the Mustang. We're just gonna lie low for a couple of days. Someone's got my money, and someone's gonna show me exactly where it is."

Ten

By Sunday morning the snow had turned into a blizzard and two feet of the white stuff was being predicted. The roads were impassable. The local radio station was announcing emergency conditions, and cars were abandoned in deep drifts all along the Thruway from Poughkeepsie to Albany.

"I won't press charges, Pete," said Joelene into the telephone. She was wearing a pair of sunglasses to cover her shiner even though it was as dark as twilight in the hall. "I told you that last night. I just want to forget Don Diamond, get him out of my life."

"Joelene?" Uncle Percy called from the bedroom.

"I'm coming! Pete, thanks for being there." She laughed. "No, I don't need a doctor, just a psychiatrist to explain what I saw in that jerk in the first place. And Pete, be careful on the roads today."

"Joelene?"

Joelene went into Uncle Percy's room. Uncle Percy was in bed with the bedside light on. He lay with his eyes shut, and his eyelids were as thin as tissue paper.

"I don't feel so good."

Joelene came over and took his pulse and felt his forehead. Her hand felt as cool as an angel's wing on Uncle Percy's brow. His lips were parched. Joelene supported his shoulders as he took a sip of buttermilk through a straw. He opened his eyes and looked at her. "You don't look so good either."

Joelene laughed, though it hurt her face. Even under the sunglasses Uncle Percy could see the shiner. Joelene took off the glasses and Uncle Percy tried to whistle, but his lips were too dry.

"Don Diamond," she said.

"I have to go to the john." Joelene helped Uncle Percy walk slowly through the house to the bathroom and slowly back again. He was unable to pass much water. His feet were swollen and he had trouble breathing. Joelene perched herself at the foot of the bed and began to massage his feet. He lay very still and Joelene thought he had fallen asleep when he said, "I don't want to go to no hospital. You promise me that, Joelene?"

"I promise, Uncle Percy."

"When my time's come, my time's come. You know what I'm sayin'?"

"I hear you, Uncle Percy."

He shut his eyes while her hands went on kneading his feet. "Good," he said.

Later, when he was asleep, Joelene tiptoed out and went to the telephone. She spoke softly so as not to wake him.

"Cousin Moira," she said, "I don't want to alarm you, but I think Uncle Percy is fading. Perhaps not today, but soon. You said everything you want to say to him?"

"Oh, Lordy, Joelene, if only I could get to you today. I can't get the car out, and I can't walk through the snow. But I can send one of the girls over."

Joelene looked out at the wind whipping the snow into a dark frenzy.

"Uncle Percy is resting real easy right now, but I just wanted to let you know, in case. . . ." Her voice trailed away.

"I'll call those that are necessary. Ondine will be over soon. Let me know if there's any change."

"I will." Joelene hung up. Then she lifted the phone again and rang the doctor. He wasn't in, and she left a message on his answering machine. There was nothing he could do anyway. She felt depressed and in need of human company. She had not wanted to wake George. He had been asleep when she came in last night, for which she had been grateful; she did not want him to see her face, not from some vanity about her looks but because the black eye represented her own guilt and gullibility. Joeline was shamed by it. And she was afraid,

afraid of what young, crazy, hotheaded George would do when he saw it. But she needed his companionship now.

She opened the door of his room and pulled on his toes. "George, get up," she said. "I want to talk to you." He sat up in bed, bare to the waist with his hair hanging over his face. Just the sight of him made her smile a little. She said, more gently, "Come on. I'll put some fresh coffee on in the kitchen."

She went through in her mind, as she ground the coffee in the box held between her knees, what she was going to say to him. How difficult it had been for her to bring him up on her own. How she had worried about her inadequacies, knowing her own mother's failures there, not in caring for a child, no one could have loved her more than her own mother, nor could she love George more than she did, but in the sensible way, in the way people seemed to judge what sensible was. Responsibility and maturity and so forth. Settled things: things like proper houses and lawn hoses that *tick-tick-tick*ed through summer days as they irrigated the gardens; and station wagons, Volvos, not orange Mustangs that could burn rubber; and barbecues that lit with one match and didn't go out; and hand-knitted sweaters à la Ralph Lauren, not hems stuck up with plastic tape. Joelene got up and put on the coffeepot. She stared out the kitchen window, seeing nothing.

A memory came back to her, sharp and acid as a wave of nausea. She was a little girl, three or four years old, sitting on her mother's knee in a yellow-flowered swing seat. She had put up her hand to her mother's throat, where five perfectly round black bruises circled her windpipe. She had asked her mother what they were, and her mother had kissed her on top of her head and said, "Love bites, child." And there had been other occasions, too, she remembered now. Shame had made Joelene try to block the memories out. With a shock she realized that she had almost repeated the same evil pattern with Don Diamond. It was almost as though she had felt she must deserve it. Joelene's self-respect recoiled. She would not be a victim. She would not. Joelene clenched the end of the counter with her hands.

How could she explain to a boy why his mother thought she had fallen in love with such a toad as Don Diamond? How could she explain to him that Don's money and gifts had made her think that despite everything perhaps here was a man who could provide for her kid? Shame swept over her, for she had discovered none of those things were important at all, and her phantom bougainvillea-covered house was just that, a phantom, compared with a ramshackle redwood house near Poughkeepsie with an old man dying in the front bedroom.

"Mom, what happened to you?" said George, coming into the kitchen and pulling on a sweater over his T-shirt as he caught sight of her eye. She took off her sunglasses and let him have a good look. A series of emotions swept over George's face: fear, recognition, anger, love. Joelene burst into tears, and he put his arms around her.

"You were right," she said, "and I was wrong." She straightened up and went to her pocketbook for a handkerchief. "I've put us all in danger through my stupidity. I've been a bad mother to you. How come you turned out so good?" She began to cry again.

"It's OK, Mom." He was distraught, but he tried to hide it. The effort it took him brought Joelene a fresh gust of tears.

"Where is Don?" he asked, pouring their coffee. His lips had set into a grim line.

"I don't know and I don't care. I never want to see him again. If he comes here, I'll call the police."

"What happened?" They sat on opposite sides of the kitchen table. Joelene put her sunglasses back on.

"It's about money, George. He thinks we took some money that was hidden in the back seat of my car."

"I don't know anything about any money," said George.

"Oh, George. My coat! Uncle Percy's microwave! Look at me and tell me you didn't buy them."

"Jesus, Mom. The guy's a crook! It's not his money. He embezzled it. He gets it from little people who pay for protection from his thugs."

"You don't know that."

"I don't know exactly *how* he gets it, but it's not legal." George sat back in his chair. "If it was legal, why doesn't he go to the police if he thinks we stole it? Why doesn't he? Because he can't; he has to come here and beat up on you to try to get it back."

"It's still stealing."

"I've done nothing wrong. I haven't spent a cent on myself."

"You'll still have to give it back."

"I can't. I've spent it."

"You've spent it? *All* of it?"

He looked up quickly. "How much was there?"

"I don't know, but it must be quite a lot for Don to go to so much trouble."

"Well, it's gone. So there's nothing he can do about it."

Joelene didn't know whether to believe him or not. She sipped her coffee and then shook out two aspirins in her hand from a small bottle and went to the sink for some water.

"How's Uncle Percy this morning?" asked George.

"Oh, George," she said turning to him, "I don't think he's going to be with us much longer. I asked him if I should call Cousin Bea in Amarillo to come and see him and he said, 'No, she hasn't come to see me in the last thirty years, why should she come now?' "

George got up and went to the shiny new microwave on the countertop. He pressed the button and opened and closed the door a few times.

"Damn old bugger," he said softly. "He's not going

to get much time to play with his new toy."

"George, I'm going to sit with him awhile. Will you be OK?" She crossed to him and stretched up and touched his hair. "You won't do anything foolish? One fool in the family is enough."

"Nowhere I can go in this weather. Nah. I'm going to do some work in the ark. There's some varnishing Uncle Percy wanted done. I could finish it in a couple of hours." George went to get a kerchief to tie around his hair.

All day long it snowed, and when George came in for a break he put his head around the door of Uncle Percy's room. I was sitting there with Joelene. George's eyes were red-rimmed, and I thought it must be the fumes from the varnish. Uncle Percy was lying quietly awake, but Joelene had fallen asleep on a chair. On her lap was a bag of Scrabble tiles. George put a finger to his lips at me as a sign not to disturb them and withdrew. I heard him going out again to the ark.

Don and Ernie froze in the barn. Their California clothes were inadequate for the weather. It snowed and snowed. Don kept going to the door and peering out the crack and cursing and then diving back into the Nissan to curl up under his jacket on the back seat. They shared a packet of honey-coated peanuts Ernie had found in a pocket and two chocolate mints, wrapped in cellophane and called Sweet Dreams, courtesy of the motel, which Don had inadvertently wrapped up with his belongings.

"Hey, boss, I've hit the jackpot!" Ernie had been rummaging around in the Mustang.

Don shot upright as Ernie's beaming face appeared at the window.

"You found the money?"

"No." Ernie held up a paper bag. "Gummy bears."

"Piss off," said Don.

"You sure you don't want one?"

Don threw himself down on the back seat and pulled his jacket over his head. He had never been so cold and hungry in all his life. When he got his hands on that kid, ooh, what he would do with him! He cracked his fingers in anticipation. He had a plan. He'd been thinking about it and he knew what he would do, but first this snow had to stop.

It snowed and snowed, and the two-feet prediction went to three and the three feet went to four. In the middle of the night the snow stopped abruptly. The wind dropped and the clouds blew away. A moon came out, high and bright as though it were deep winter instead of fall, and made the whole countryside look like a Currier and Ives print.

No one saw it, because everyone was asleep. Everyone, that is, except Uncle Percy, who lay awake in his room and watched the clouds scudding by, illuminated. But they were not clouds he saw, they were animals, polar bears and elephants, lions and emus, monkeys and doves, giraffes and anteaters. He watched them till the dawn came and he wanted to go with them, but not yet. Not yet, Uncle Percy. There was one last thing he had to do.

Eleven

The next morning Don woke early. He was stiff with cold, and his stomach growled with hunger. He was struck with how quiet everything was and then he sat up, shivering, and realized that the snow had stopped. He got out of the back of the car and stretched and then huddled his shoulders back in to conserve warmth and ran to the doorway. His breath froze in the air. He pushed against the door but couldn't budge it. He climbed onto the hood of the Nissan, hooked his fingers over the top of the barn door, and pulled himself up high enough to look through a twelve-inch gap at the top. The light was glaring, and it took a minute for his eyes to stop watering.

And then, as far as he could see, he could see nothing but snow. They were lost in a sea of the damn stuff. Their tracks of Saturday night were no longer visible. Don couldn't even see the road. The snow had drifted up against the door of the barn to the height of a man. No wonder he couldn't budge it.

He jumped down and banged with his fist on the top of the Mustang.

"Ernie, get up. Get up, goddam it! We've got to get out of here!"

Ernie crawled out, looking mournful and wrinkled. His cast hung heavy on his arm.

"Whatcha want me to do, boss?"

"I'm gonna stand on the hood over there, and you're gonna stand on my shoulders, and I'm gonna hoist you through that gap. You can try to open the door from the outside."

Ernie looked appalled. "Me, boss? I've got a broken arm."

"All right, Ernie. Would you like to get up on the hood and I'll stand on your shoulders and you can try to squeeze *me* through?"

Ernie's 135 pounds looked at Don's 200 pounds. He sighed. "OK, boss."

Don and Ernie climbed on the car and Don knelt down while Ernie climbed on his shoulders. Don grunted as he staggered to his feet. Ernie held on to Don's hair.

"Let go of my hair."

"Sorry, boss." Ernie leaned against the wall and gingerly got to his feet. Don wobbled beneath him and then got his hands on Ernie's calves and pushed upward.

Ernie grabbed the top of the door with his one good arm and Don shoved again and Ernie managed to get one leg over the top of the door. "One, two, three!" said Don and shoved again, and Ernie screamed and disappeared over the top of the door.

He landed with a thud in the middle of a snowdrift. He stood up and fell down and stood up again.

"Hey, boss!" he shouted. "How am I supposed to move this stuff?"

A shovel hurtled over the door and landed like a javelin in the snow beside him.

"Uh, thanks."

"You're welcome."

In twenty minutes of sweating and panting, Ernie managed to clear enough snow away to open the door for Don to get out.

"Boy, this stuff's heavy," said Ernie.

The men stood up to their thighs in soft snow. Don shivered with cold and kept blowing on his knuckles. The sun was high and glistened off the surface of the snow. Ernie began to giggle and threw a snowball at Don.

"Hey, cut that out," said Don. "I'm thinking." He put on his aviator sunglasses.

"I thought you had a plan?"

"Yeah, but now we ain't got no car. We ain't got *two* cars. Which way's the main road?"

Ernie pointed in the direction of a copse of trees in

the distance. Don set off, floundering and falling in and out of the drifts. Ernie floundered and fell behind him.

"We going back for the Merc?"

"Too dicey. Ernie, why'dya have to pick a barn so damn friggin' far off the road? This stuff's gonna ruin my shoes. Ruin 'em."

The telephone in the hallway rang.

I was in the shower and didn't hear it. Monday had been declared a snow day, so there was no school.

Joelene was sitting on Uncle Percy's bed with a bowl of Quaker Oats in her hands. She had made it in the microwave and served it with brown sugar and thick cream poured over it. She had discovered that Uncle Percy had a sweet tooth.

"Honey, why didn't you ever put a telephone in here beside your bed?"

"Never got around to it."

Joelene put the bowl on the tray and went to answer the phone. "George!" she hollered. "It's for you!"

Uncle Percy heard George clatter out of his room. Joelene came back in. She opened up his pill bottle.

"I had them already."

"Hello?"

"Have you?"

Uncle Percy realized they were both trying to listen to George's conversation.

"Right on," they heard him say. "Anytime today. . . . Great." He hung up. Uncle Percy and Joelene looked at each other. George clattered back into his bedroom.

"Hate those sandals," said Joelene.

"Don't his feet get wet?" asked Uncle Percy.

The phone rang. Joelene waited for George to get it and sighed and got up again and went to answer it.

"George!" she hollered. "It's for you!"

"Gee, thanks, Mom."

"Hello? . . . Yeah, that's right. . . . Sure. . . . Okie dokie. Anytime today." He hung up.

Joelene, who was leaning in the doorway of Uncle Percy's room, watching him with her arms folded, said, "George? Can I have a word with you?"

"Sure. Hi, Uncle Percy. You feeling better today?"

Uncle Percy grunted. "Reckon He's too busy to deal with me right now."

"George, what are you up to?"

"Nothing. Why?"

"You want to tell me about 'Nothing'?"

"Nothing to tell. Could I have a word with Uncle Percy? Alone?"

Joelene knew when she was defeated. She squinted at her son through her good eye. "Don't tire him," she said. She took the tray away. Uncle Percy had eaten only two spoonfuls.

"Anything I can do for you, Uncle Percy?" George asked.

"Just get my chest to stop hammerin' away."

"Would it bother you if I went way out back and did some target shooting?"

Uncle Percy leaned back into his pillows. "Used to have fun skeet shooting back there with my dad. In the fall we used to have skeet-shootin' parties on Saturday afternoons. Leaves burnin'. Sky blue as you ever saw. Clay targets spinnin' like birds in flight." Uncle Percy put his hands up, palms out, in front of his face and looked at them as though he had never seen them before. The sun coming in the window hit them and made them pinkly transparent. "I can see my bones," he said.

George held his own hand up beside Uncle Percy's Uncle Percy glanced at him as though he had forgotten he was there.

"About the rifle," said George to remind him.

"I promised you, didn't I? Take the rifle, and remember, don't go holdin' your breath when you shoot and aim a little lower to compensate for the bullet rise."

George took the rifle from under the bed, still wadded up in the oily sweater, and Uncle Percy stretched out a hand and touched it like an old friend.

"I want you to have it," he said. "Ain't no use to me no more."

"Sure it is," said George.

"No use foolin' ourselves." He shut his eyes and George felt dismissed and left.

Joelene came in and began tweaking the covers and plumping things up.

"You've got visitors coming," she told Uncle Percy.

"Who?"

"Moira and someone else who just flew in, Cousin Bea from Amarillo. I stayed with her one night on the drive over from California? She has a real nice ranch house with a sunken living room right off Route Forty."

"She must think I'm about to croak."

"Uncle Percy, that's not worthy of you."

"It's the truth, though. And don't let them go touching any of my goddam stuff." He glanced around the room and motioned at the blue folder that stood on the bedside table. "Hide it behind my piller," he said.

"They're kin, Uncle Percy." But she hid it behind his pillow anyway. "Besides, they're good women. Far better than me. Sensible. Dependable. And they don't get involved with folks like Don Diamond."

"No fun," said Uncle Percy.

"Some fun," said Joelene, looking at him with her black eye. "I'm going to try and put a bit more cover-up on it," she said. "Don't tell them what happened. Say I walked into a door or something."

He thought, when she was gone, how like her mother she was. Except the hair, of course. No woman of his era would have had hair that California gold color. Well, perhaps Ginger Rogers. But she was a movie star. One expected them to be different. But their voices, the slight breathy drawl—why, he could shut his eyes and believe that this Joelene was *his* Joelene. Norman's wife.

And their energy, yes, in that they were alike too.

Joelene Mathieson never stopped working. Every time he left his room he saw some other little change she had made. He could hear her humming now all over the house, opening doors, rustling papers. She shouted out questions to him, but he knew he did not have to answer. It was an ongoing conversation taking place regardless of walls, regardless of time. Joelene Morgan had done that too. He and Norman would be sitting on the porch and Joelene would be in the kitchen or down below in the vegetable garden, her beloved vegetable garden, chattering away a dime a dozen. They had been the happiest times of his life.

"Why, Pericles Morgan, you are looking extremely fine today, extremely fine."

Uncle Percy was caught unawares. His sister-in-law, Beatrice, stood in the doorway. He had been so engrossed in his memories that he had not heard the car pull up. Behind her, Moira was stamping snow off her boots.

"Come and help me with the coffee," said Joelene to Moira. "I want to show you how the dress for Pauline turned out."

Bea shrugged off her coat in the hall and hung it on one of the hallstand's protrusions.

"Nothing changes," she said.

She came back in and stood looking down at Uncle Percy in his bed for a few minutes and then she leaned over and hugged him so hard Uncle Percy knew he must be looking like death. He could hardly breathe until she stood up again, and he adjusted his eyeglasses, which had gotten skewed.

Uncle Percy looked at Bea. He hadn't seen her for thirty years, and she looked just the same. She was still the ugliest woman he had ever seen. How Arthur, bless his dear departed soul, had ever climbed on top of her, he could not imagine.

"The Lord be with you," said Bea as she leaned over again and kissed him on the forehead. Uncle Percy immediately felt guilty for his thoughts. But then Bea had always made him feel guilty.

"And also with you. Sit down, Bea," he said, trying to make up for it.

Bea shifted a pile of clothes and papers off the one chair in the room and placed it close to the bed. Her spaniel eyes in her long mournful face examined his. He supposed it was her lugubrious expression that made her seem so ugly to him, because taken individually her features were quite ordinary. They were not out of kilter or anything. But she was Martha to Mary, Laurel to Hardy; he had never seen her smile.

Bea pursed her lips and settled carefully on the chair beside the bed. Bea was probably only twenty-three or four years older than Joelene but it may as well have been a hundred. Bea had always looked thin and parched. Her blouse was pin-tucked, with a Peter Pan collar. It was the kind she had worn to college when she and Arthur met. She had always dressed this way: sensible shoes, thick stockings, a pleated skirt, a helmet hairdo that sat square above her unadorned face. Bea's bangs hadn't changed since she was seven years old. She couldn't be a day more than sixty.

"Why, you're just a chicken," said Uncle Percy out loud.

I was standing in the doorway and Uncle Percy saw me and called me in. Bea took a big ball of knitting wool out of a bag at her feet.

"This place hasn't changed, Percy, since you and your brothers lived here."

She began to ply her needles with an expert fast hand.

"Still got the country store on the corner, I see."

She went on knitting what seemed to be a blanket of enormous proportions.

"Still got the Inn," she said.

She sighed.

"Arthur hated this place."

"That's why you went to Texas."

"He hated the lumber business."

"There wasn't much Arthur did like."

"Well, you never did like Arthur either. I never knew three brothers who fought as much as you three did. I have to blame my mother-in-law for that. She told me once how, when you were very young, she brought home a small wooden stable with carved animals for Norman's birthday and how you tried to destroy it."

"It was an ark, not a stable."

"Don't argue with me, Percy, I know what I'm talking about. The light just shone out of Norman for her. He was her golden child. You and Arthur never could match up to anything he did or said." She kept hitching up the length of knitting under her right arm as though the weight was too heavy for the needles. She turned her knitting.

Uncle Percy shut his eyes and let her talk on. He imagined it was Joelene talking away in another room and he didn't have to answer.

"How are you getting on with George?" said Bea. "When they visited, he reminded me a lot of Tom, a no-hoper if ever I saw one. 'Joelene,' I said, 'why don't you get George to cut his hair? Looks like a girl.' 'I can't get him to do it,' she said. 'Then make him, make him do it,' I said. 'Cousin Bea,' she said, 'it just isn't that important. I'll pick my own fights with George.' "

But Uncle Percy had drifted away. It was summer thirty years ago and he was in the garden double-trenching a bed for Joelene Morgan's vegetables. Little Joelene was away on a sleep-over with a friend. Uncle Percy remembered he had his shirt off, and the late setting sun was beginning to cool his skin. Norman had been drinking all afternoon, bottles lay around his chair in the sun, and when Norman drank he became bad-tempered. He said something to Joelene as she went by with a colander to pick some beans for the evening meal. She was wearing a thin cotton skirt, he remembered, and no shoes, and the late-afternoon sun silhouetted her legs as she walked past his brother. She made some flippant remark to him and he threw a bottle at her and it hit her on the shoulder.

Percy saw him do it and slowly put down his shovel. "Stay out of this, Percy," Norman had shouted. He lumbered to his feet and grabbed Joelene by her long brown hair. He yanked back her head.

"Let me go!"

"Stay out of this, Percy."

"Let her go." Norman and he had stared into each other's eyes and Norman had let go Joelene's hair and she had run crying into the house.

"It's your house," said Norman, "you're the eldest brother; you tell me to leave. But you can't, can you? You can't because you're in love with Joelene." Percy swore at him and Norman had just laughed and staggered out to his truck and drove down to the Inn.

Later that night Percy had woken up. He heard sounds through the thin walls that he had heard before. He had lived in the same house as his sister-in-law for seven years and he had heard a lot of different sounds through the walls: the sounds of lovemaking, the sounds of anger, the sounds of reconciliation. He had heard the creak of a bed, the gasps and moans, and celibate Percy's imagination had filled with forbidden thoughts.

Thou shalt not covet thy brother's wife. It was impossible not to hear them, but he had trained himself to turn over and fall asleep. This night, he could not ignore them.

He heard Norman's shouted angry words, the jagged crash of a lamp hitting a wall, the sound of Norman beating Joelene, thuds into soft flesh that made him clench his teeth and fists. He heard Norman grunting and Joelene whimpering. He put his hands over his ears, but he was unable to shut them out. "Percy! Percy!" Joelene screamed. "For God's sake, Percy, help me!"

Percy grabbed his rifle from under the bed and threw himself into his brother's room. He flung himself onto his brother's back. Norman was naked as the day he was born. He was much bigger than Percy, but he was soft. They rolled off the bed and onto the floor and Norman was wrestling the rifle from Percy, but Percy managed to roll free and the rifle barrel swung up under Norman's rib cage and went off. "You bastard," said Norman, as his hands fell off him. They were the last words he said. It had all happened so fast.

Uncle Percy's lips were parched. He opened his eyes. He would have liked a sip of water.

"But then," Bea was going on, "we all thought it was a good idea to ask Joelene to come here to look after you. I don't know what magic words Moira used to get her to come, but they worked." Bea shook her knitting in amazement. "And when you think"—she began to stumble over her words, dropped some stitches, and went back, picking them up like specks on a surface—"when you think, um, about Norman, what happened . . ."

"I shot him."

Bea's fingers began to fly over her work, and she flashed a glance at me.

"Not in front of Ondine, Percy."

"I shot him," he said again.

"Well, yes, you did. But Arthur always said it was an accident."

"I meant it." A tear glistened on Uncle Percy's lower lid. It sparkled behind his glasses and began to slide slowly down his cheek. Bea stopped knitting and stared at it.

"I'm going to die, Bea."

"Oh, what nonsense. We're all going to die one day."

Just then George came lumbering in with his lank hair over his face, his stooped shoulders looking cold and narrow under a matted pea jacket he had rescued from the hallstand.

"Hi, Cousin Bea," he said, shoving the rifle under the bed. He stood up and put his hands in his pockets, aware that he had interrupted something. "I've got a surprise for you, Uncle Percy."

Uncle Percy looked up at him. George saw the dampness on his face and took a handkerchief from his pocket and leaned over and unconcernedly blew Uncle Percy's nose for him.

"What damn thing are you up to now?" said Uncle

Percy, with a good clearing sniff of the nostrils.

"Look out the window."

George hoisted Uncle Percy up—he weighed only as much as a child—so he could see out the window. A delivery truck was being unloaded and Parrish was supervising. A shiny new wheelchair was carried across the snow and deposited at the front door. Parrish wheeled it in.

"What do you think?" said George. "You said you hate staying in bed." Uncle Percy eyed it with suspicion.

"Rubber wheels," he said.

"Yep," said George, going over to it and sitting himself down. "Great suspension." He moved it backward and forward in the narrow space. "No more supermarket carts for us."

"Where'd you get this, George?"

"You may not believe this, Uncle Percy, but I am paying for this myself. I've got a job. At the hardware store." Uncle Percy's eyes lit up. "Six bucks an hour. All day Saturday. Forty minutes for lunch, and I don't have to cut my hair."

George gave Uncle Percy a sip of water. Uncle Percy squeezed his hand.

"Now, how about a spin? I can fold it up in the back of your truck and take you wherever you want to go."

"I'd like to go to Gimlock's."

Joelene and Moira brought in a coffee tray.

"Did I hear Gimlock's?" said Moira. "You're not

really going to take him back to the hardware store, are you? Joelene, you wouldn't let him, would you?"

"Honey, if Uncle Percy wants to visit Gimlock's and he feels up to it, I'm going to let him go."

Joelene offered Uncle Percy some buttermilk, which he sipped gratefully. "You up to it, Uncle Percy?"

"Reckon I might be. I'll need a little rest first."

"You just say when you're ready, Uncle Percy," said George and left the room.

Uncle Percy put his hand over Joelene's hand as she held the glass up for him to drink.

"I'm going to die."

"Yes, Uncle Percy. But I'll be here."

Uncle Percy took another sip and waved the rest away. He lay back on the pillow with his eyes shut and a smile on his face.

"He's asleep," said Joelene, and we left the room quietly.

In the hallway Joelene glanced through the panes at the side of the door. A brown UPS delivery van was parked across the road. It reminded her of something.

"Hmm," she said. "I want to ask George some questions."

But George was in the shower, his tape player belting out some music, so she had to wait for another opportunity.

° ° °

Bea and Moira were staying for lunch, and Moira, knowing that Joelene's talents in the kitchen rose to Chef Boyardee on toast or reheated frozen offerings from the supermarket, had brought along what she called "the makings." A big pot of fragrant risotto was being prepared at the stove.

Moira believed that all problems could be solved by food, and going by her girth one could be forgiven for assuming that Moira had gone through a lot of sorrows. But the truth was that Moira was happy. At least she kept telling us so and, being her daughter, I believed her. I watched her frying onions and garlic and stirring in the rice. She really was happy. She believes all that stuff in Ephesians—you know, wives submit to your husbands, children obey your parents, slaves obey your masters. It's enough to make a feminist gag, but it works for her.

Cousin Bea is a different story. Cousin Bea, I've heard my dad say, was never satisfied. Bea was into building up treasures on earth; she was not afraid of moth and rust. That's why she had scooped Arthur out of Poughkeepsie and the lumber business and worked to put him through law school all those years ago. They had moved to Texas, but it turned out not to be the land of milk and honey she had expected. The only thing that turned out was that Bea produced four daughters and Uncle Arthur developed a dicky heart and died when he was only fifty years old. "He just wore himself out," said my dad.

"Wore himself out." This said as he stretched for another beer can and slumped down to watch Sunday football on television.

My dad represented a whole other branch of the Morgan family—Uncle Percy's father had a much younger stepbrother, Alexander, who was my father's father—you don't have to understand all this, but Moira thinks it's important. Next to her Founding Membership Card of The Miss Manners School of Etiquette, Mom carries our genealogical tree on three-by-five index cards. Her own family is not half as interesting, she says. Anyway, Bea took seniority, as it were, on anything to do with Uncle Percy, even though it was usually Moira, and now Joelene, who did the actual work.

"You don't realize what you have until you lose it," said Bea as Mom tossed a salad and Joelene set the table.

"Poor Uncle Percy," said Joelene. She had done a remarkable job with the concealer, and her eye looked only puffy.

Bea put her forearms on the table and clasped her hands in front of her. "What I mean is," she said, "has Uncle Percy made a will?" Her spaniel eyes looked glumly at Joelene and Moira.

Moira turned from the stove with a wooden spoon in her hand. "Why, I never asked him," she said. "I didn't think it was my place."

"You have to be practical, Moira," said Bea, moving her elbow so Joelene could set down her cutlery.

"There's this house," she went on, "and the land. There's all his possessions, his car. What are we going to do with them?"

"What does he want us to do with them?" said Joelene. She put the salad on the table. Bea served the steaming risotto to all of us.

"Of course," said Bea, "even better, from a monetary standpoint, would be if Uncle Percy signed over his possessions now."

"Why?" asked Joelene.

"Probate. You'd avoid it. When Arthur died the girls and I couldn't get our hands on anything for months. There was money in the bank, but it was in Arthur's name and I had to borrow money to buy food. The widow is the last one they think about. You know all about that, Joelene. Why, if Tom had been a better provider, if he had thought ahead a little about what might happen to you and George, you wouldn't be in the situation you are in now."

"What situation am I in?" said Joelene without rancor.

"Oh, Bea," said Moira. "Eat up."

But Joelene knew what situation she was in: she had nothing, but it hadn't seemed to matter before. "Uncle Percy does hate the IRS," she said.

"He's probably got money salted away all over the place," said Bea as Moira helped her to seconds. "We'll never find it. The government will get it all. Tell that to Percy and see how he feels."

"Well, what do you suggest we do?" said Moira.

"I suggest we find the deed to the house and the registration papers for the truck and have Uncle Percy sign them over to whomever he wants to have them."

"He'll hate doing that," said Joelene. "It would be like—like him giving up."

"I've never seen any papers," said Bea. "Uncle Percy is so secretive about those things. I wouldn't know where to begin looking for them. Where would we find them? Joelene, have you seen them?"

Joelene thought of the blue folder and her filing.

"I might have," she hedged.

"Then the sooner we find them the better," said Bea, standing up. "I hate untidy ends."

Joelene felt they were talking about Uncle Percy as though he were some recalcitrant ball of wool. "I'll take him in some food," she said. "We could ask him then what he wants to do."

"Rice," said Uncle Percy when he saw the risotto that Joelene took in to him. "I hate rice." Joelene went to get him a glass of buttermilk.

"Percy," said Bea, sitting on the edge of his bed and taking up her knitting again, "this is very difficult, but we need to know if you want anything special done."

"Done when?"

"Well, after you've gone."

Uncle Percy did the tortoise thing with his neck, which if Bea had been with him more she would have recognized as a danger signal.

"I ain't goin' anywhere."

"Don't be stubborn, Percy. I'm only trying to put things in order."

Moira was standing with her arms folded in front of her, looking very uncomfortable. Joelene didn't want to be there and kept hovering in and out of the door until Uncle Percy said, "Stand still, woman."

"Percy, when Arthur died—"went on Bea and got no further.

"When Arthur died? Died? You think I'm goin' to die now, you ugly old bitch? Croak right here in front of you? That why you came here, Bea? All the way from Amarillo to Poe-kipsie to see what's in it for you? *Well, I'm not going to do it just because you want it. I'm not going to make it all neat. It's going to be untidy. Damn right.*" Uncle Percy shut his mouth in a tight fine line so his lips disappeared. He shut his eyes and turned on his side away from Bea.

"I'm only saying," said Bea, standing up and rolling up her knitting and putting it away, "that we should be practical."

Uncle Percy didn't move or blink. The whole line of his slight body was like a reproach. Bea swept out of the room with Moira and whispered to Joelene as she took her coat from the hallstand, "If you find those papers, Joelene, you must get him to sign them. It would save so much trouble later on."

Moira put her arms around Joelene. "You call me now

if you need me. You coming home, Ondine?"

"I'll stay awhile."

Joelene closed the front door on them and went along the hall.

"Joelene!"

"Yes, Uncle Percy?" She stood at the foot of his bed.

"Have they gone?"

"Yes."

"Vultures." He coughed and Joelene came around and helped him sit up.

"It ain't easy," he said. "I lost control."

"I know."

"You know what she's talking about?"

"Bea wondered if you had a will. She said you should sign over the deed of the house and the . . ." Joelene faltered.

"And the what?"

"The ownership of the truck." Joelene began to cry softly. "I know where the papers are, if you want them." She took a tissue from a box on the side table.

"Sit me up," he said. "Swing my legs out of bed." Joelene did so. He nodded toward the small table they played Scrabble on. Joelene brought it forward and then took from the blue folder the papers he needed. She had known exactly where they were. She placed them in front of him and handed him a pen. He took it with trembling fingers.

"Uncle Percy?"

"I'll do it. I'll do it. Just a minute."

Joelene stood for a minute and then she left him sitting there, staring at the deeds and the registration papers. She saw him pick them up and look at them as if he had never seen them before. Then he put them down and she left the room. She telephoned Moira, who had just arrived at our house.

"I can't do this," she said. "I just can't do it."

Twelve

Outside, in the brown UPS delivery van, there came a small sound.

"Will you look at that?"

"What?" Ernie tripped over the trussed-up body of the driver in the back of the van.

"Careful, careful," said Don, moving to one side as he let Ernie look through the rear window.

"I don't see nothin' but a minibus."

"Yeah, look at that friggin' bus. 'The Peter Pan Community Home Bus.' Jesus. It's brand new, Ernie! You told me yourself you took the other one and how old it was. Look at it. That's my friggin' money paid for that!"

Outside the community home seven or eight people jumped around with excitement. Parrish skipped and ran along the road to Uncle Percy's, hurdling over banks of snow that had been pushed up by the morning's road plow. Parrish took only a cursory glance at the parked UPS van as he bolted into Uncle Percy's house. A minute later he was back, dragging George by the hand and shouting, "Come and thee! It'th a miracle! No one knowth where it came from."

"I sure know," said Don, slumping down inside the van and gnawing at one side of his thumb. "We got to get George," he said to Ernie. "He knows where the money is."

"How d'you know? Perhaps someone took it while they were on the road."

"Just look at his friggin' face," said Don.

Ernie, peering through the window, saw George and the others examining the bus. A smile of pure satisfaction and delight shone out of George's face as he denied to the others that he knew anything about the origins of this magnificent gift.

"Yeah," said Ernie, slumping down beside Don on the floor of the van, "he knows, all right." Ernie was wearing the brown uniform of the driver. Don was still in the rumpled clothes of yesterday.

"I think," said Don, "that the money is hidden right there somewhere. Somewhere in that goddam house. We got to get inside."

Ernie stood up and took another peek through the window. "Oh-oh," he said and slid down again.

"What is it?"

He whispered, "Cops."

The trussed-up driver, his mouth sealed with tape, began kicking his heels against the side of the van.

"Stop it," said Don and hit him across the side of the head with his gun. The driver passed out and lay still again.

Don stood up and peered out the window.

"It's that boyfriend of hers and a trooper. Jesus, don't we get any breaks? Ernie, let's get out of here. Nice and quiet, now. We'll come back later when there's fewer people about."

"We think he might still be in the neighborhood," Pete was saying. "He hasn't been back to the motel, and the Mercedes is still there."

"We've got someone staking it out right now," said the trooper, Frank O'Malley. "If he comes back for it, we'll grab him."

"I'm scared," said Joelene. They were sitting in the kitchen. Pete put his big hand over Joelene's where it lay on the table.

"It's OK, Joelene. If he comes near you again, I'll hit him so hard he'll fly back to California without a plane." He squeezed her hand.

Frank O'Malley said, "You sure you don't know anything more about this money?" Joelene thought of George and shook her head. "You've told us everything you know? If he still thinks you've got it, he'll be back."

Joelene shook her head.

"Lay off, Frank," said Pete. "She's told you everything she knows."

Frank got to his feet. "I've got to get back. Anything happens, anything you remember, you call me."

"I will. Thanks."

"You coming, Pete?"

Pete stood up and went into the hallway with him. "No, I'll stay here for a few minutes and get a ride later."

When the trooper had left, Pete turned to Joelene. They were both standing against the kitchen door and he put his hands on her shoulders. "I'm getting mighty fond of you, Mrs. Joelene Mathieson," he said. "I don't want anyone hurting you."

"Oh, Pete, don't complicate things." She stamped her foot.

Pete tipped back her head and kissed her.

"We just did," he said. "I want to talk to George."

"He's avoiding us. He was here until Parrish ran in wanting to show him the new bus—" She stopped abruptly.

"A new bus?" Pete nodded and looked at her. "Now I really want to talk to George . . . if that's OK with you, Joelene?"

She nodded.

"I'll go find him," he said, kissed her again, put on his Stetson, and left. Joelene went in to see how Uncle

Percy was doing. He was still sitting the way she had left him, his big swollen feet planted on the floor and his head hanging heavy in his hands. The papers lay unsigned on the small table. He was brooding. He looked up at her when she touched him on the shoulder. It seemed as though his eyes had sunk farther into their sockets.

"Can I help?" she said, kneeling down beside him. She put out her hand to take the papers away but he stopped her.

"Never knew what to do about this house," he said, staring down at his feet again. He was very short of breath. "Know what to do now. Put my house in order." He looked up. "Cain't give it away, Joelene. Not before. But I can do something. You get me dressed, Joelene, and call my goddam sister-in-law to drive us into town."

George saw Pete's long lean figure strolling toward him from Uncle Percy's house. He had a good idea what Pete was coming for. George was no fool, and he knew he didn't want to talk to Pete.

He thought quickly. "Come on, Parrish, let's go for a ride in this thing. Anyone else want to come?" A whoop went up, and six or seven of Parrish's housemates scrambled into the bus.

"Hey!" shouted Pete. "Wait a minute! I want to talk to you, George."

"Quick, quick," said George, hurrying Parrish and jumping in behind the driving wheel. He switched on the radio, loud, reversed the van, and took off with a jolt away from Pete's running figure. George looked in the wing mirror and saw Pete standing with his hands on his hips in the middle of the road, looking perplexed. George let out a deep breath of air.

"Where are we going?" shouted Parrish above the *boom-boom* of the radio.

"Anywhere. Let's find that goon who beat up my mother."

"Bathtard," said Parrish.

"Let's start at the motel. Maybe they know something."

Pete came back to the house and found Joelene dressing Uncle Percy. Uncle Percy kept saying, "Just a minute, just a minute," and resting in between.

"Do you really want to do this?" said Joelene. Uncle Percy looked at her like a very fierce pixie.

"OK," said Joelene and slipped on his shoes. "As long as you've made up your mind." She stood up.

"Joelene," said Pete, taking her aside, "I've got a very bad feeling about all this. I don't want you in this house alone, and I don't think this house should be empty." He coughed and said, "Would it bother you if I moved in for a while till they catch this guy?"

"It wouldn't bother me at all, but do you really think he'll come back?"

"Yes, I do. Can I ring my office and let them know where I'll be?"

"Of course. I can make up a room for you upstairs, except it's freezing up there."

"It's not too warm down here."

She laughed. "You'll get used to it. Uncle Percy has disconnected all the heating up there, though."

"I can put up with it."

Joelene went to put on her red plush coat. Pete touched the fabric softly and looked at her with his lips pursed.

"You think George has the money, don't you?" said Joelene.

"What do you think? Where'd he get the money to buy this?" He stroked her collar.

"And Uncle Percy's microwave."

"And the minibus."

"Oh, Pete, what can I do? In a way I agree with him—oh, you know. If I had found that money I wouldn't want to give it back to Don Diamond either. But it doesn't belong to us. We have to turn it over to the police."

Moira's car tooted in the driveway.

"That's Moira and Bea. We're taking Uncle Percy in to see a lawyer and Dr. Beamer."

"Let me look through the house while you're gone. I

might find the money, and then we can make a deal with George or Don to leave you alone."

Joelene nodded and Pete went and picked up Uncle Percy in his arms and took him out to the car. Joelene pushed the wheelchair out and they folded it into the trunk.

"See you when we get back," said Joelene. She blushed as she said it. She thought there was something comforting, domestic, about the idea that Pete would be there in the house when she returned. Moira drove off, and no sooner had she turned out of Broad Street than a brown UPS delivery van turned into it from the other end.

"What if they recognize me?"

"How can they? They ain't never seen you properly."

"I'm scared, boss. Perhaps you should do this. What if I get caught? I'd end up in Sing Sing. I'm still on parole! They'd throw the book at me."

"Ernie, how can I go? You think Joelene would let me near the place? She'd call the police before I got to the front door."

Ernie touched the false mustache he was wearing with nervous fingers. He was wearing the brown uniform and cap of the delivery firm.

"Now you know what to do," said Don from his seat in the back of the van.

"Yeah, I know," said Ernie, pulling on the hand brake and picking up his clipboard. He had got very good at doing things with one hand. "I'm to say, 'Delivery for Mr. Morgan,' and insist on his signature, and that way I can get a good look around the house, get into his room maybe."

"Keep your eyes open," said Don, handing over a large parcel. Ernie took it and jumped down into the snow.

He went up the steps of the porch and rang the doorbell and waited. He went over his words. He peered through the panes beside the door and nearly turned and ran when he saw not Joelene, not George, but Pete coming to the door. A thin line of sweat prickled up above his mustache.

The door swung open and Pete stood there.

"D-delivery for Mr. Morgan," said Ernie, pushing the clipboard at him.

Pete looked at him seemingly without recognition and then signed his name. Ernie shoved the parcel at him and backed off.

Pete looked after his hurriedly retreating figure. Something about him struck his memory. An arm in a cast. The man at the diner. Mike had said he had his arm in a cast.

"Hey," said Pete. "Just a minute." But the little man had broken into a run. He got to the van and jumped in. Pete started after him. The van took off with a jerk and accelerated. Pete lunged after it and managed to grab hold of the handle of the back door. The door swung open and for a second Pete was face to face with Don Diamond. Then Don pushed the trussed body of a man in his underwear out of the back door, and Pete and the man rolled onto the road as the van swung crazily along Broad Street and disappeared around the corner.

George and Parrish, et alia, had drawn a blank at the motel. The red Mercedes still sat in solitary splendor in the parking area and, yes, Mr. Diamond had been friendly with a small man who had taken another room a week before him. A Mr. Doe. Yes, John Doe. The girl at reception did not think this was an unusual name. As for Mr. Doe's car registration, he had kept changing cars, always complaining about them at the Avis counter, so they had given up keeping a tab on the license plate. Now, would they excuse her as she was busy? Half the motel was undergoing reconstruction.

The Peter Pan members were desolate as they walked past the demolition dumpsters in the forecourt. "I know," said George. "Let's go and get some ice cream at the mall." This immediately cheered everyone up and they drove off to the mall. While Parrish and Sam and Laetitia and Hank were trying to decide between rum raisin and double chocolate, George picked up a pamphlet in the store. He stood stock still as though he had been struck by a bolt of lightning, and Parrish had to ask him three times what he wanted before he heard. George decided he didn't want ice cream, after all, but bought a carton of Heath bar crunch to take home. He handed Parrish the pamphlet as they walked back to the van. It advertised the circus, which was setting up at the showground for Halloween.

"They alwayth come at thith time," said Parrish, as he bit into a double scoop of rum-raisin ice cream. "My brother workth there. He loveth animalth."

George stopped and took Parrish's face in his two hands. He puckered up and kissed him on the forehead.

"I love you, Parrish. One day I'll count the ways."

"I nearly had a heart attack," said Ernie over his shoulder as he drove like a maniac along the Thruway. "I knew he would recognize me." He hit the driving wheel with the palm of his hand. "I knew it. I knew it."

"We got to ditch this van," said Don. "Take the first turnoff." They zigzagged over a number of roads and crossed the Taconic once or twice, not knowing where they were going.

"Oh, no," said Ernie, as familiar trees and streets began to appear. "Oh, no! We're back in Poughkeepsie!"

They circled the derelict mall in the center of town and turned up Main Street.

"Stop right here," said Don.

"Right here, on Main Street? I'm blocking traffic."

"Delivery vans *always* block traffic. Just get out with a package and your clipboard and keep walking. I'll go the other way and meet you over at McDonald's in five minutes. We need wheels."

Ten minutes later, over a Big Mac, Don came up with an idea. "The money's in the house. Right?"

"Right."

"And there are too many people in the house for us to get in quietly. Too much trouble if the cops come."

"Right."

"We got to get the people out of the house."

"How?"

Don squeezed extra mustard and pickles over his burger. Ernie winced as he watched him taste it.

"George. We take George and hold him at the barn. Either he tells us where the money is or they come and get him."

"How'd they know where to look?"

"We'll tell them. Either way we get our dough back. Pass the pepper."

"Boss, that stuff must do terrible things to your stomach." Ernie was feeling queasy. Nothin' had gone right with this deal. Nothin'. He was going to end up back in prison. He could feel it. Ernie shivered and sipped at his Coke.

A mail delivery man came in sorting out a pile of

letters. "Mornin'," he said, as he handed over a stack of envelopes to the guy behind the counter. Ernie and Don watched him go out and climb back into his postal delivery truck. They looked at each other.

"Yeah," said Don, "that might work." He got up, wiping his mouth on a paper napkin.

"Oh, no," whimpered Ernie. "It's probably a federal offense."

On the last Monday of every month there was a dance at the firehouse. Tickets were three fifty each, and that included a glass of really sticky sweet punch. Peanuts and popcorn were extra. There was no alcohol, but the men used to sneak out and walk down to the Inn for a refill every half hour or so. The money went to support the Volunteer Firemen's Activities Committee.

Gerry and Mike had roared up to Uncle Percy's front door to deliver a message that George was at the dance and would be back late.

"He's avoiding us," said Pete to Joelene when they'd gone.

"And you found nothing in your search today?"

"Nope. I turned the house upside down, and there's no sign of the money."

"Perhaps we made a mistake. A b-i-g one. Perhaps there isn't any money."

"Oh, Joelene," said Pete. "Face it. Why do you think

Don and his sidekick risked coming back here today? They think the money's here too."

Joelene sighed and then sneezed as she blew some dust off a book. Uncle Percy had fallen asleep and Joelene and Pete were in the front parlor sorting through the accumulation of Uncle Percy's seventy-seven years. The parlor was more like a storeroom. Joelene had been going through a trunkful of old books and linens. She had thrown a book at me—"Hey, bookworm, you might enjoy this"—and I had settled down in a corner with an illustrated story about the early days along the Hudson River Valley.

Joelene found an old schoolbook with spidery copperplate writing in it. The edges of the book had been nibbled by mice.

"What I Want to Be When I Grow Up," she read, *"by Pericles Morgan."*

She settled back on her haunches on the floor. Pete went on picking through old clothes and shoes and putting them in some kind of order. Under a rust-colored inside-out sweater he discovered a glass and a plate with a congealed substance solidly cemented to its surface. He threw them into a black plastic garbage bag.

"When I grow up I want to be an engineer and build bridges that cross the Hudson River and the Mississippi. Men on barges and ships will look up as they sail under them and wonder at them."

"Kid had dreams," said Pete.

"We all did. What did you want to be when you grew up?"

"Me? Oh, not much. Go into the kind of business I'm in, I guess. My dad had an apple orchard up near Schuylerville. Not much money in that." He threw another crusted artifact into the plastic bag. "Can't get people to pick apples anymore around there. Isn't that a fact? I tried to run the orchard for a while after Dad died, but it was backbreaking work." He paused. "It ended my marriage."

"Ah," said Joelene, suddenly busying herself with a whole stack of dusty volumes.

"We had a kid too. A girl. Never see her now. She lives with her mother—she remarried—in Pennsylvania. It was easier just to give her up, drop out of her life."

They worked in silence for a moment. A car went by outside, and then the silence surged backward.

"And what about you?"

"You know most of it, Pete. But I had dreams, still do."

"The house with bougainvillea?"

She laughed and threw back her head so he could see her strong little throat. "I'll take it with wisteria," she said.

He glanced at her still swollen eye. "How about quitting?"

He helped her to her feet. She wiped some dust from

her jeans and pushed up the arms of her sweater.

"You like some hot chocolate, Ondine?" she said.

"Sounds good to me."

Later, as I lay in the spare bedroom, I heard the sounds of Pete walking through the house. I heard him check the front door and look in on Uncle Percy. I heard him climb the stairs behind the kitchen and go to bed. The sounds comforted me and made me feel protected. Joelene must have felt the same way, the way she was when she was just a little girl playing in the potato patch. I dreamed about her that night and slept so soundly that I didn't hear George letting himself in later with his key and tiptoeing to his room.

The following day dawned as clear as a bell and I had to go to school. The sky was high and blue and the few birds that had not migrated south yet were trilling their heads off.

Uncle Percy was wide awake when Joelene went in to him.

"Feel stronger today," said Uncle Percy, as Joelene helped him into the wheelchair to take him to the bathroom. But he felt as frail and fragile as one of the singing birds under her fingers.

"Got to get into the ark today," said Uncle Percy as he waited in the kitchen for breakfast. He said he'd like some bacon, but a piece the size of a postage stamp seemed to overwhelm him, and he drifted off into some inner contemplation as Pete came down the staircase.

"Can you give us a makeshift ramp, Pete, so I can get Uncle Percy's wheelchair down the steps and into the ark?"

"No problem."

"Good morning," said George, arriving with the vigor and appetite of youth at the kitchen table. "Boy, have I got a surprise for you today, Uncle Percy."

Uncle Percy looked up and smiled. George was the only one for whom he smiled like this. It even sparked some of his old venom. "What goddam thing you up to now?"

"You have to wait and see," said George, pouring a bowl of cereal for himself. Joelene threw on some eggs and more bacon for him and Pete.

"Allow me," said Pete, taking over the frying pan. He had heard of Joelene's prowess in the kitchen. "We do a lot of this at the firehouse."

"Are you a fireman or an insurance salesman?" said Joelene, pouring everyone some coffee. Pete grinned but said nothing.

"Whatever you're up to, George, it better not cost me a penny," said Uncle Percy.

"Not a nickel," said George.

Joelene and Pete looked at each other. "George . . ." they both said.

He threw up his hands and tossed back his hair. "Don't attack me all at once."

He switched on the radio and gobbled down his food

still standing and then microwaved a carton of ice cream. He spooned the softened ice cream into his mouth.

"You have to tell us where you've hidden it, George," said Joelene.

"Hidden what?"

"Stop pretending. We know you've got it." Joelene kept glancing at Uncle Percy. She did not want to mention money in front of him or worry him about the strange goings-on around the house with Don and the Man with the Broken Arm.

"Mom, I don't want to lie to you. So why keep asking me?"

"You're putting her in danger," said Pete.

"How'm I doing that?" said George, tossing the empty carton into the kitchen bin. "If I *did* know, wouldn't it be safer *not* to tell you?"

"It doesn't belong to you," said Joelene.

"It doesn't belong to him either. Look, I've got to go and get something. I'll be back in an hour. Uncle Percy?" He squatted down beside Uncle Percy till they were at the same eye level. Uncle Percy's crooked fingers gripped his arm like a lemur's delicate paw. George whispered into his ear, "Genesis six, verse nineteen." Uncle Percy's eyes lit up like they had the first time he heard Jerry Garcia on the headphones. "You wait," said George and ran out of the house to the van where Parrish was waiting.

"He's all right, that boy," said Uncle Percy.

° ° °

An hour later Joelene was pushing Uncle Percy around the ark. It was a cold day but the sun was streaming in from the opening above them, piercing the gloom like a great spotlight.

"Take me up," said Uncle Percy, gesturing toward the elevator. "I'll show you how it works." Up they went with a jerk and a jolt to the third deck. Joelene kept her eyes shut until the elevator stopped. She felt humbled that Uncle Percy trusted her enough now to show her around.

"It's beautiful," she said, wandering around the polished deck and examining the stalls and the cribs, the fine carpentry and the carvings. Uncle Percy took a carved pineapple out of his pocket. "This is the last one," he said. "George made it." He showed Joelene where it went, and Joelene stretched up and slipped the dowel piece into place. "Now it's finished," he said.

"Not quite," said George, appearing suddenly to them from the deck above.

"How did you get up there?" said Joelene.

"I scaled it from the outside. I've rigged a rope up here. Uncle Percy, watch this." George swung another rope forward and slid down to join them. He went to the mechanism that operated the drawbridge. The portcullis was suspended above it, the chains freed from their earlier confusion. George had moved some of the sandbags from the metal counterweight and tied them to the chains closer to the gate.

George pressed the button to operate the drawbridge, and the drawbridge began to creak open. He grinned at Uncle Percy. "It works," he said. The huge wooden bridge opened slowly and the sunlight thrust in farther and farther until, with a sudden thud, the drawbridge stopped and they could see they were at the level of the leafless trees at the top of the slope where the old lumber road went past.

There was a grinding, metallic noise, and the earth shook, and Joelene went white until she saw it was not an earthquake causing it but a red mobile crane moving into position. It let down its pads, telescoped its arm, and after a few minutes' delay swung a large metal plate across the gap between the drawbridge and the road.

"Hot diggity!" said Uncle Percy, straining his neck forward. Joelene pushed him nearer to the entrance, and that's when they heard the music. Up from Broad Street came the sound of a marching band, with the *boom-boom* of a big bass drum and yours truly on the trombone. The whole of the high school band was there, and the smaller children made up a percussion choir with cymbals and a snare drum and tympani and triangles and bells. Up we came with Tolley's Circus and a man with a monkey and an organ who played sweet music completely out of tune with the rest of us. But it didn't matter as we clattered over the metal plate and onto the drawbridge and led the way into the ark and saw Uncle Percy's shining eyes.

"Oh, when the saints"—*clash, clash*—"go marching in"—*clash, clash*—"Oh, when the saints go marching in"—*clash, boom, clash.*

"Oh, my, my," said Joelene.

In behind us came the ringmaster, and behind him came the circus people and with them came the animals. There were two llamas led by a boy; six white horses with colored plumes on their foreheads; four dancing brown bears in jeweled collars who twirled solemnly as they walked; and a woman with two doves on her head who carried a cross on the arms of which perched fourteen vivid, fluttering, blue, green, and red parrots. There were jugglers and clowns and acrobats and a man with a hoop and a string of small white poodle dogs that jumped and rolled and walked on their hind legs.

"Bichons are so clever," said Joelene, until a small black-and-white terrier did a double somersault into the hoop. "And so are mongrels." The school band switched into the first of its Sousa marches. Uncle Percy's eyes didn't leave the troop that poured into his ark. A mother giraffe and her baby swayed elegantly into view. The baby ran around like a foal on legs that seemed too long for it. The mother's head came in first, followed by her long neck and then her body until she stood near the center of the ark where the deck gave way to the sky.

A television crew walked in backward, filming the

arrival of George's pièce de résistance. There was a huge trumpeting sound followed by a squeal, and a pair of young elephants, fat, gray, wrinkly, and odorous, shook their way over the ramp and into the ark. The keepers sat on their backs, their legs tucked under the flapping ears, and twitched commands at them. The trunk of the larger elephant unrolled and quivered, its big pink nostrils flaring, over Uncle Percy in his wheelchair. It dropped its inquiring tip to his hands, and Uncle Percy touched the soft, wet, quivering snout and felt the blast of air as the elephant breathed out.

All the townsfolk had arrived, attracted by the procession. I never knew so many people still lived in this backwater off Poughkeepsie. They had come from everywhere like children following the Pied Piper. Parrish and Laetitia had brought their pet rabbits to join in, and Moira and Bea, having been warned what was to take place, were also there.

The band had played all through its repertoire, and now we swung back to the beginning again. Uncle Percy looked slowly all around his ark—his creation—and saw it full of animals and people, smells and noise. He breathed in deeply and smiled at George across the throng. He had never imagined in his wildest moments that he would see it thus. It was like manna to his soul. It nourished something in him that he thought had died long ago. Even now, as he had come to terms with his death, the joy around him breathed like a flame at an ember. But he had a covenant to keep. Uncle Percy shut his eyes and found the thought no longer painful. He opened his eyes and took Joelene's hand and when she leaned down to listen to him, he said, "Remind me to tell you something." And then the ringmaster came and saluted Uncle Percy and we all began to leave the ark, two by two, over the drawbridge, and Parrish came skipping down the side of the lumber road and blew me a kiss and I gave him an extra blast on my trombone.

An assortment of circus transports was parked down on the street opposite the redwood house. As I was putting my trombone in its case and was about to jump onto the school bus with the band, I saw Parrish acting peculiar. In among all the people still milling about, he was circling a small electric-powered postal delivery van that was parked behind a horse float. I thought that was odd, because we don't get mail deliveries here anymore. He crouched down, his red baseball cap on his head, a rabbit under each arm, and bit his fingernails.

"What is it?" I said, going over.

Parrish whispered. "Thothe men, they're the oneth." He was looking around for George, who was probably somewhere paying for all this out of his secret hoard. "We've got to thtop them."

The elephants were the last of the animals to turn off the lumber road and approach us. Parrish's brother was one of the handlers. Suddenly Parrish thrust the rabbits at me and ran along to meet the elephants. I shrugged and went to his house to put the rabbits back in their hutch.

When I came out I was just in time to see Pogo, the larger elephant, backing up and sitting down on the postal van. Then Pogo let out a trumpet of noise and sat back even farther and raised his front legs, and the van crushed like an aluminum can under him. Two men scrambled out of the van on all fours, picked themselves up, and ran like Keystone Cops down the middle of the street and out of sight. Everyone thought they were clowns. Parrish was laughing so hard he had to sit down himself and that's where George found him, with tears running down his face, pointing hysterically down the street after the disappearing figures.

George helped Parrish to his feet and they ran for the Peter Pan bus and roared off in front of us. We set off at a more sedate pace in the school bus, singing an interminable version of "Miss Merry Mack-mack-mack, all dressed in black-black-black."

Thirteen

George and Parrish didn't return home. Not that afternoon, not that night. Joelene spent the night sleeping fitfully on a chair in Uncle Percy's room. Uncle Percy's breathing was harsh and painful. Pete tried to make her go and rest but she refused, and by morning Uncle Percy's condition was unchanged and there was still no word of George or Parrish.

The police had been notified and a check had been made of all road accidents and admittances to hospital emergency rooms but nothing turned up, which at least was some comfort. Of the blue Peter Pan bus there was not a word. It had simply disappeared. In the morning, Frank O'Malley telephoned to say that Don Diamond's red Mercedes had been blown up in the night.

"On purpose?" asked Joelene when Pete relayed the story to her. "Why? Who?"

"Frank says some real professional goons were seen at the motel last night."

"How could it happen? I thought there was a stake-out."

"Yeah, I did too, but they got to the car, we think. The girl at reception saw them."

"They looked like Colombians," said Mike Astanazy, who had dropped by to pick up the pumpkins and candles for the Halloween party that night.

"You saw them too?"

Mike picked his teeth with a Stim-U-Dent and pumped his powerful little arms under his leather cycling jacket.

"They ate at the diner. One had Chuck's chicken wings with Texas hot sauce and the other had tacos with beef chili and jalapeños." He picked at a particularly stubborn shred between his teeth. "He complained about the chili."

"And they blew up Don's car?"

"They probably set a timer on it," said Pete, "and were halfway back to wherever they came from when it went off."

"It was a sign to Don Diamond. Next time *he'll* be in the car," said Mike.

"Perhaps they meant him to be in it, and it went off by mistake," said Pete.

"If they touch my boy . . . if they touch one hair of his head . . ." said Joelene. Pete put his arms around her.

All day people came in and out of the house bringing the cold chill air of the outdoors with them. The sky was gray and yellow and drops of melted snow spotted the wooden floor of the hallway, but Joelene was grateful to be busy and preoccupied. She stared at the phone, willing it to ring, but it stayed sinisterly quiet.

Moira and Bea visited after shopping. They had bought hot dogs and beef patties and hamburger buns and colas for the kids' party at the firehouse that night. They stayed for an hour with Uncle Percy and suggested that Joelene and Pete get out for some air. Pete called Lars to come up and sit with the women while they were out, and Joelene shrugged into her red plush coat and was grateful to get out of the house. She was depressed about Uncle Percy and worried about George and Parrish.

They walked through the tree-lined streets under the sullen sky and up to the overpass and hung over the parapet watching the traffic on the Thruway below. Joelene had once felt a kindred spirit with these people in the cars and the trucks and the buses, all going somewhere, anywhere, but somewhere different.

For many of them, there had to be somewhere better than the place they had been. Joelene knew the feeling, and her mother had known it too. She knew these people because she had been one of them. They had dreams too—of bridges that spanned rivers, and chandeliers that twinkled in perfect houses, and lawns that were

forever green, and apple orchards that got picked—and wanting to be something, be someone, and being unsure how to achieve it, they had mistakenly assumed that motion, action, restlessness must bring it about. And even if that frenetic traveling, zipping along the Thruway or the Taconic, whooshing under the overpass on which she stood, even if it didn't bring the dream about, why at least it stopped one from coming too close to the awful contemplation that it might not be possible after all.

Joelene pulled her coat tighter around her as she leaned against the parapet with Pete. Her eyes searched the whizzing lanes of traffic for a blue bus, a sign, an arm waved out a window. Hello, there, I'm here. It seemed Joelene had always lived near a main highway. She could remember lots of them, overpasses and cloverleafs and loops and els. Always close to a route for escape. When George had been small, she would push him across a nearby bridge and stand with him watching the traffic flow by. When a diesel-fueled juggernaut would come into view, little George would put up his hand and pull his arm down sharply two or three times and the drivers would respond by hooting their horns for him before they belched away beneath his feet. Joelene shivered.

"You cold?" said Pete. "Let's go home," he said, taking her arm.

The gray afternoon dragged on, and by nightfall the

first firecrackers started sounding around the town and the first trick-or-treaters started wandering up and down the street.

Joelene was beside herself with worry and to take her mind off it had set up her Scrabble board on the tray table at the foot of Uncle Percy's bed. She and Pete played across his toes.

"It's not like him not to phone," said Joelene, looking at her tiles. "What if Don does have him? What if he hurts him?"

"If he has him, we'll find him. All the guys are out looking for them. We've just got to sit here—"

Joelene jumped up. "Oh, I can't. I can't. Why, oh, why did George take the money? Why did he spend it like that and draw attention to himself?"

Uncle Percy, whom they had thought was asleep, suddenly said, "He did it for me."

Joelene flew to his side. "Oh, Uncle Percy, I didn't mean it like that. I loved the animals yesterday!"

"Best day of my life."

"But now George is missing, and Parrish." She took out a packet of gummy bears from her jeans pocket and nibbled on one. "I must be the most stupid woman in the world. Gullible. Naïve. Hell, I feel dumb. I have never been able to see through people. I believed what he told me. How could I have trusted Don Diamond? How? I could kick myself when I think about it. He's a toad. He's vicious. He'll stop at nothing to get what he wants. Oh, poor George!" She burst into tears. Pete rose to comfort her, but she shook her head and came over and looked at her tiles again. "Canetoad," she said picking them up and building on Pete's "D" for "dorsal."

"Is that allowed?" he said, staring at it. "Two words?"

"It depends how you say it," said Joelene. "Cane toad or canetoad."

Pete laughed, and even Joelene had to smile. Two yellow plastic clips sat like butterflies in her hair. The phone rang. They both got to it at the same time.

"Hello?"

"This is the AT and T operator. Will you accept a collect call from Mr. George Mathieson?"

"Yes!"

"Mom . . ."

"George, honey, are you OK? Where are you?"

A man's voice. "Joelene, we got your kid."

"Who is this? Where's Don?"

"I'm tellin' you for Don. You bring us the money and we give you George."

"I keep saying it, I don't know where the money is!"

"You find it. Listen carefully. I'll only say this once. You come to Stewart's Barn . . ."

He began to give directions, and Pete nodded to indicate he knew where it was.

"One more thing. You talk to the police and your boy's done for." He hung up.

° ° °

"How'd I do, boss?"

"You did good, Ernie. Good." Don Diamond's eyes searched the street for any sign of movement as they came out of the telephone booth. Don Diamond looked terrible. Gone was the impeccable dude of four days ago with his knife-pleated trousers and his polished shoes. Four days of living in a barn and running for his life had reduced him to a shambles. When the Mercedes had blown up and he knew how close the Colombians were, he had reacted as though a jolt of electricity had been passed through him. Don Diamond had gone into shock. He had nearly been killed!

If he hadn't thought there was something suspicious about the car when he went back to try to get it last night, if he hadn't followed his own animal instinct that something was terribly wrong, he would be dead. He had stood in the shadows of the blinking blue and red neon of the motel—VACANCY, VACANCY—and known. Something was wrong! His nostrils had flared. His ears had flattened. He had decided not to approach the car in the open. He crept around the courtyard and in an unmarked car saw a young cop, sound asleep, his head thrown back and his mouth open. Don knew he was a cop even from this distance. He could smell one a mile away.

He had crawled along in the dark, searching for something to use as a tool, and had found a wire dry cleaner's hanger on the ground. He had twisted it straight, found another, added to it. Then in a pile of building debris behind the motel he had found a long strip of wood, like a lath, and had fashioned the wires to the end of it.

Don crawled back to the car, knelt on one knee about fifteen feet away and delicately, carefully, tried to insert the end of the wire into the door lock. Each time he missed and the wire fell tinkling to the ground he broke into a sweat. The lath wobbled and teetered and swung in his hands. It was almost impossible to keep it steady, and just when he was about to give up, and had told himself that he was imagining things and should just go up and stick the key in the lock, the wire caught. He held his breath and then gave a tiny, infinitesimal jab from the end of the lath and *boom!* the car exploded in his face and he was thrown backward off his feet, blinded by the flash.

The orange light of the flames lit the whole courtyard. The cop came running, his arm up to protect his face. People came staggering out of their motel rooms in their pajamas. But Don Diamond didn't wait to see. He crawled on his hands and knees into the shrubbery like a wounded animal.

When Don had caught his breath and his sight came back he found he was shaking. Chaos reigned in the courtyard as he hobbled away into the darkness. He was heading for Ernie, waiting somewhere near in the blue minibus. The bus was too hot to stay with, but now they had to get away before the Colombians realized they had missed him. Don was breathing heavy and dragging his leg when he suddenly bumped into Ernie running across his path.

"Jeez," screamed Ernie. "You scared the daylights out of me."

Don snarled. "Where the fuck are you going?"

"I—I came to look for you, boss."

"Then you're running the wrong way."

"I heard the explosion. Jeez. What happened? I thought you was dead."

"Well, I ain't. Suckers haven't got me yet."

Ernie began to whimper as they ran and ducked and weaved their way back to the minibus. "I don't like this, boss. I don't want to go back to prison." He whimpered again. "I don't want a Colombian necktie."

"Shut up," snarled Don, as he reached the driver's side. He was still shaking so hard he could hardly open the door.

"You drive," he said, pushing Ernie into the driver's seat.

"Where we goin'?"

"To the railway station. We got to get a taxi."

Don Diamond caught a glimpse of himself in the rear-vision mirror as he got in the passenger seat. The whole front of his hair had been singed off.

"Shit," he said, touching the bristly stubble that was left. "I've lost my friggin' hair."

Don put a hand up to it now as he went back to the taxi and hauled George out of the back seat. George's hands were tied and his mouth had been sealed again with tape. Parrish had been left tied up at the barn.

Don pulled a sheet over George and threw one to Ernie and donned one himself. Holes had been torn for their eyes and mouths. "Now we walk," said Don, hooking his hand through George's arm. They were one street parallel to Broad Street. Distant firecrackers and the squeal of excited children reached them. Fireworks exploded in the sky and the air was sulfuric and cold. They passed a group of children dressed as goblins who shouted, "Trick or treat?" but Don groaned and snarled at them so realistically that they scattered shrieking in front of them. They kept to the shadows, crunching over the snow with their breath vaporizing, and approached the redwood house from the lumber-road end.

Joelene had said goodbye to Pete on the porch and he had taken off for the barn. He had alerted Frank and the others, but they would wait until he got there. He had called Buddy to come up from the firehouse and stay with Joelene until he returned. Buddy had promised to be there in ten minutes. They could hear the sounds of the party over the telephone. Joelene watched a red and gold sunburst of light in the sky and then turned around and went back inside, locking the door behind her.

"I think it's going to snow," said Joelene as she went to Uncle Percy.

"I want to visit the ark," said Uncle Percy. His eyes were unfathomable, milky as the sea after a storm.

"It's so cold out there, Uncle Percy." Joelene shivered.

"One last time," said Uncle Percy. "I cain't sleep with the noise of the fireworks."

Joelene stood looking at him for a moment, undecided.

"All Soul's Night," he said. "All Hallow's Eve."

He looked so soon to be among that blessed throng himself that Joelene wrapped him in his blanket and helped him into the wheelchair. When she had his socks and shoes on, they went down the ramp and along the boards that Pete had laid to the door of the ark. Each time a firework bloomed over them in red or blue, the shadows of the scaffolding fell across them like heavy black beams.

"I've forgotten a flashlight," said Joelene. "I'll be right back." Uncle Percy nodded. Joelene ran back into the house and was just reaching up to the top of the refrigerator where a big yellow industrial flashlight stood when she heard footsteps on the front porch. She thought it was probably Buddy and went to the hallway to let him in, only to see dimly through the panes of the front door the looming form of a white-sheeted ghost. She hesitated and then she heard a key being put to the lock and then being dropped and an oath being uttered and she knew it was Don Diamond.

Joelene spun around, grabbed the flashlight from above the refrigerator, then on the spur of the moment, picked up a small paring knife from the sink draining board and let herself quickly and quietly out the back door. Her heart was beating so loudly and the blood pounding through her ears that she thought Don would hear and come running after her.

"Hurry, Uncle Percy," she said. "Don is back."

Uncle Percy showed her where to put her fingers to open the door and she pushed the wheelchair through it and closed it behind her. A new, stout bar leaning against the hull could be used to barricade the door from the inside and as she dropped it into place she was grateful for Uncle Percy's penchant for secrecy.

She pushed the wheelchair over to the elevator.

"I want to use the staircase."

"Not now, Uncle Percy," whispered Joelene. Uncle Percy shook his head and gripped the arms of the chair to stand up.

"Uncle Percy, Don is out there." Joelene could feel the veins in her neck knotting. But it made no difference. Uncle Percy struggled to his feet, his legs wobbling under him, and took a step.

"Going to meet my maker on my feet," he said.

Joelene glanced over her shoulder. He raised his voice. "But yea, Lot's wife looked back and she turned into a pillar of salt."

"Ssh," said Joelene, but Uncle Percy's voice thundered out. "And the voice I had first heard speaking to me like a trumpet said, 'Come up here, and I will show you what must take place after this.' " He took another step.

"OK, Uncle Percy, OK. But we must be quiet until someone comes." She put her shoulder under his armpit and held him up. She switched on the flashlight, and they shuffled slowly toward the staircase. In the gloom it was like a minaret in front of them. It rose gracefully up and up until its top disappeared into the clouds. It was Jack's beanstalk, Rapunzel's tower, a spiraling, open fantasy. It was Uncle Percy's stairway to heaven.

Slide, together, pause; slide, together, pause. They reached the first step and Joelene saw in the flashlight's beam that carved on each riser was an angel blowing a trumpet.

On the first step as he stopped for breath, Uncle Percy said in his normal voice, "I loved your mother, Joelene."

"Yes. She told me."

"She was a pure thing."

"You were her friend." They stepped up. A crackle of fireworks spluttered from somewhere distant. The staccato sound of small explosions followed. Uncle Percy was silent, and Joelene listened to his labored breathing as they stepped up again.

"I have to sit down," he said.

"Can't you make just one more step?"

"Just a minute. Just a minute." Uncle Percy's legs

began to buckle under him and Joelene lowered him down. She sat beside him in the huge darkness.

"It won't take much longer," she lied, wondering how she was going to get him up to the top, her ears aching from listening for Don to come crashing through the door.

"No, it won't take much longer at all," said Uncle Percy.

"Tie him up," said Don. They were in Uncle Percy's bedroom. Ernie threw George onto a chair, tore a strip off the sheet he had worn, and wound it around him. They began ransacking the place. They turned over the mattress and ripped the stuffing with a knife. They emptied the drawers and the suitcases and swept everything off all the surfaces and the tops of the shelves. Joelene's neat attempts at filing were emptied onto the floor. They had just pulled up the floor rug when they heard a man's voice outside shouting, "Joelene? It's me, Buddy."

Don and Ernie froze, then Don jerked his head at Ernie and he nodded and ducked behind the bedroom door. Buddy knocked on the front door, turned the knob, and came in. Passing the open door of Uncle Percy's room on the way to the kitchen, he glanced in and saw George gagged and tied to the chair.

"George!" he said. George gargled through his gag and rolled his eyes to try to warn him, but it was in vain.

Buddy came rushing into the room and Ernie hit him on the back of the head with his gun. The two men tied him up and strapped his mouth shut with strips of sheet and went back to their work. They were methodical. When they had demolished everything in Uncle Percy's room, they moved into Joelene's next door. George heard them dragging and crashing things and then the unmistakable sound of a hundred potatoes thudding and rolling over the bare boards.

George struggled with his bonds. He had to get help. With his bound feet he began to kick at Buddy's prone figure on the floor. *Come on, Buddy, wake up. Wake up.*

On the second flight of stairs, Joelene noticed that the risers were decorated with dragons and beasts. The dragons had seven heads and great long tails that stretched from one side of the steps to the other. Around the dragons Uncle Percy had carved a multitude of stars. As for the beasts, they were an amalgam of animals: the body of a leopard, the mouth of a lion, the feet of a bear. They too had seven heads. Bits of scripture came back to Joelene as she and Uncle Percy rested again. Uncle Percy's hands dangled down between his legs as they sat on the stair. His breathing was so labored that Joelene wanted to tell him that she was taking him right back into the house, Don or no Don, but when she looked at the fine, bent head, the effort he was putting into this last final act to control his own life, she couldn't say it.

"How long did all this take?" she said instead, moving her flashlight along the carvings. In the beam, she saw Uncle Percy's fine fingers outlining the carved shape of a locust. It was like watching a blind man reading Braille.

"Most of my life. I had a lot of empty nights. Most of these I carved before I even thought of building the ark."

"Why did you build it, Uncle Percy?"

His fingers paused. "Cain't rightly say." He was silent, catching his breath again, and then he said, "Wooden prayers. Never was much good with words. Could recite the scriptures, but that's about it. Couldn't ask for forgiveness."

Joelene put her hand on Uncle Percy's arm. "Forgiveness for what?"

Uncle Percy groaned. It started as a low moan and then it grew, like the bellow of an animal in pain, into the deepest, most mournful sound Joelene had ever heard.

She whispered again, "Forgiveness for what, Uncle Percy?"

"I killed him. I killed your daddy, Joelene."

"It was an accident."

"Oh, they say. They say. They didn't know what was in my heart. But I knew. I knew. I wanted to do it. I'd thought about it often enough."

Joelene drew Uncle Percy's hand up into her own. It was as cold as marble.

"My mother told me you saved her life."

"She never blamed me for taking him away from her?"

"No."

"You never blamed me for growing up without a father?"

"I never knew any better." She laughed softly. "Uncle Percy, I had a wonderful life. Mother and me, we were happy. We were like gypsies, pirates; the highways were our sea lanes. We had nothing and we had everything. She made it all an adventure."

"Is that right?"

"That's right." She rubbed his hand in hers to warm it. "We forgave you long ago, Uncle Percy."

A loud crash sounded from outside, and Joelene stopped rubbing Uncle Percy's hand and listened. Was Don trying to come in the door? There was another crash and the sound of splintering glass, and she figured it was coming from the house. But soon Don might come looking for her, and here she was exposed on the staircase with no protection and Uncle Percy dying. And where was George? What had Don done to George? Joelene ground her teeth as she thought about that. It might be half an hour or an hour before Pete came back from the wild-goose chase Don had sent him on. Anything could happen in half an hour.

"Uncle Percy, we've got to get you up to the animal deck."

"Yes, that's where I'm going."

"Do you think you can make it? Give me your arm, then, here, over my shoulder. Oh, you're light as a feather, Uncle Percy." He trembled like a bird in her arms. "Oh, Uncle Percy, just another step, one more step." In the end she bent down and lifted each foot for him. They were agonizingly slow.

Don was in a rage. He was in the glass veranda and had picked up Uncle Percy's toolbox, which was not locked, and all the tools had fallen out onto his foot. He threw the box at the window and it crashed through to the yard with a splintering sound. There was an old prefabricated closet at the end of the veranda and he threw things from it in a frenzy: bloated cans of sauerkraut, ancient coats and jackets, boxes of books and pamphlets for every gadget Uncle Percy had ever bought, fishing rods and cartons of spent bullets, cleaning rods and half-used cans of paint, a stepladder, a broken vacuum cleaner, a chain saw, a kettle barbecue.

"It ain't here, boss," said Ernie. He was covered in dust and grime.

"This is the last room." They had gone through the upstairs in record time.

"It's got to be," said Don, wiping his big nose with

an oily finger. He looked a mess and he knew it and hated it. He glanced upward and saw a small trapdoor. The veranda was single-storied and above it was a small crawl space.

Don moved the stepladder into position.

"Get up there," he said to Ernie. Ernie hesitated for a moment and Don aimed a kick at him and Ernie then scurried up the steps and pushed the trapdoor up. A cloud of dust sifted down on them.

Ernie coughed. "I can't see a thing," he said. Don went to hunt for a light with a plastic bulb guard he had seen in the hall. A spider disturbed by Ernie scuttled across the ceiling. Ernie shrieked and then remembered himself and leaned nonchalantly against the top step until Don returned and handed up the light. Ernie switched it on and poked his head into the crawl space. A musty smell of mice and cobwebs met him. He swiped a cobweb from his face and Don growled below him. Ernie hitched himself up on his good elbow and lay on his stomach in the narrow space. Mice scrambled squeaking away from the light. Ernie shuddered. "Jeez, I hate this job," he muttered to himself.

They had reached the deck where the stalls stood shining and expectant and where still the faint smells of elephant and giraffe hung in pockets of the air. Joelene had made Uncle Percy as comfortable as possible on the floor where they could see anyone approaching from the staircase or crossing the floor of the hull. They could not see the whole of the floor clearly because it was pitch black down there, and even if they could, because of the angle of the decks, they could not see the door from which they had entered. It was bitterly cold and their breath hung in front of them. Uncle Percy leaned against the wall of one stall with his head back.

"Did you see him?" he said.

"Don? No."

"No, the boy."

"There is no boy, Uncle Percy." Joelene felt the hair on her scalp rise.

She touched Uncle Percy's shoulder and in the dim light from the sky she saw that his eyes behind his spectacles were open. "You're cold," she said. She took off her plush coat and placed it around him. She shivered and put her arms around herself and touched the paring knife she had slipped into her shirt pocket. Such a paltry weapon. Don would kill her before she could even make up her mind to use it. Where was Buddy? What had happened to George? Joelene's mind worked frantically through her options. There was no one to help her now. If Don came in here, she would have to protect herself and Uncle Percy. Joelene rubbed her head in anguish. As her eyes grew accustomed to the gloom she began to see two or three heavy shapes swaying over the void. I am going mad, she thought, hobgoblins and ghosts and boys that aren't here. . . . She was afraid to switch on the flashlight. What if Don was hiding below? What if she saw something she didn't want to see? She shook Uncle Percy.

"Uncle Percy," she whispered, "can you see over there? What are they? What is it?"

"Cain't see, Joelene. Has he come?"

She shook him harder. "Uncle Percy. Uncle Percy. Is there something hanging over the space?" Her voice came out harsh but it got through to him.

"That's our system. George and me. We fixed the weight of the . . . of the portcullis. . . . Jammed . . . sandbags . . . iron . . ."

Joelene stared into the space and let out a little giggle of relief. Hobgoblins? They were sandbags, heavy sandbags, to take the weight of the portcullis off the chains of the drawbridge. George had mumbled something about it to her, but she hadn't been listening. Just sandbags. Joelene sat and stared at them awhile and then got up and paced up and down well away from the edge. Heavy sandbags. *If* Don came in, *if* she could get there and cut the bags free, *if* Don was underneath . . . at least it could buy them time until someone came. Joelene listened carefully and then took the risk of switching on the flashlight. She shone it on the sandbags and then she shone it upward, following the ropes. There was a wooden beam that crossed the ark from one side to the other. If she could get on the beam and cross over, she could wait until Don came right underneath. . . . Joelene broke into a sweat just picturing it. I can't do it, she thought. I can't even sit in the balcony at the movie theater without wanting to throw up.

"Joelene!" Don's voice, muffled but loud, shouted up at her and made her heart jump. He hammered on the outside door. "I know you're in there. I'm going to count to sixty, and if you don't come to this door, I'm going to break it in."

Joelene ran back to Uncle Percy. He had heard Don too. His eyes looked at her with concern.

"Don't worry, Uncle Percy. I know what to do. You just sit tight now, you hear?" She kissed him on the forehead; his skin was as dry and taut as parchment.

Joelene switched on the flashlight again and followed the beam to where it met the hull. The light picked up the glimmer of a rope. A rope? Oh, thank God for George and his climbing, thought Joelene. She left the big flashlight with Uncle Percy and went to the wall. A length of looped webbing hung down. Each loop was a foothold. *As long as I don't look down,* she said to herself, *I might be able to do it.*

"OK, Joelene, you asked for it." Don's voice came at her hard and angry. There was a thudding, pounding sound as he began to batter at the door with a sledgehammer. The ark withheld him like a fortress. Joelene took hold of the webbing and placed her foot in the first loop. She climbed up two feet and felt for the next toehold. *Don't look down, Joelene,* she said to herself. She slipped the toe of her sneaker into the next loop and flattened her stomach against the hull. *Don't look down.* She began to spell out her instructions to herself. *D-o-n-t l-o-o-k d-o-w-n.*

Fourteen

In Uncle Percy's bedroom, Buddy had managed to hook his mouth gag on the doorknob and pull it off and had bitten his way through the sheeting that bound George's hands. George was free at last and ripped off the tape across his mouth and winced and rubbed his jaw from side to side to get the feeling back into it.

"Buddy," whispered George, untying the bonds as fast as he could.

"What happened?" asked Buddy.

"Ssshhhh! No time to explain. Get the guys here."

"Where are you going?"

"Get them to come to the ark. Quick." George sprinted for the back door and then changed his mind and dashed through the front. Buddy staggered to the telephone in the hall and picked it up. The line was dead. He pulled the phone up and saw the cord had been cut. Buddy ran to the house next door to use the telephone but there was no reply as he banged on the door. Everything was in darkness. He looked along the street and saw that every other house was the same. They'd all gone to the party at the firehouse. Buddy buttoned up his coat and began running toward the village square.

The beam had seemed so wide, Joelene thought, as she lay full length along it and inched forward on her thighs. Now it seemed as narrow and precarious as a ledge on a mountain. She kept her eyes directly in front of her. She saw every dim splinter and whorl of the wood. She dare not let her eyes wander off it. The beam was her anchorage; the thought of there being nothing underneath her but sixty feet of air made her stomach turn over. Her hands were clammy on the rope. One more inch. She heard the splintering sound of Don and Ernie at the door as it began to give, and a whining rocket from the firehouse party soared above her and lit everything up inside the ark for a brief moment and made her feel giddy. She was within arm's reach of the ropes that held the suspended sandbags. If she could just reach out now, just stretch out a little, perhaps she could touch one of the ropes. Joelene froze. She squeezed her eyes shut. Every fiber in her body screamed at her: Don't do it! She was afraid of falling. One more inch.

There was a final splintering crash and she heard her

name bellowed. "Joelene!" Joelene's head came up. They were in. Joelene took out the paring knife and reached for the rope. She could see her arm silhouetted darkly against the emptiness and the puny little knife winking as she turned the blade. She couldn't reach the rope. She inched her body farther out to the edge of the beam until her shoulders lay off it. Now. She stretched, and the tip of the knife touched the rope, and the sandbag—heavy as it was—moved and for a horrible lurching moment, because she had not expected it to move, she thought she was falling. She pulled her arm back in and clung to the beam as though it were rocking beneath her. Her gorge rose, and she put her head down between her arms against the wood and hung on until her stomach quieted.

"I know you're in here, Joelene." Don's voice sounded down below her. "And I'm not leaving until I get my money." He fired off a shot from a pistol, and it whined past and thudded into a wall. Joelene shivered and waited until she felt it was safe to raise her head. She had to look down. She had to see where he was. Joelene rolled her head over until one eye could see to the bottom of the hull. Her eyes swam as the hull seemed to tilt and right itself and she dug in harder with her hands. She saw them. They were carrying a light, a bare bulb on the end of an outdoor cord.

"Jesus, where is she?" said Ernie. "This place gives me the creeps."

She could see them clearly. They had their guns

drawn and were moving slowly into the center of the ark. Joelene bit her lip and stretched out toward the rope once more with her knife. The rope was thick, and she began to saw at it with the small sharp blade.

Up above, unseen by all of them, George had managed to scale the outside of the ark. He had crept around the ark to the tree where he and Parrish stashed things and he had picked up his rifle. He had taken off his sandals and slung the Winchester over his shoulder on a makeshift strap. He had just reached the very top of the ark when he had heard the pistol shot and his blood froze. He pulled the rope up behind him, reattached it, and rappeled swiftly and lightly down onto the animal deck.

He landed softly and crept along to where he could see Uncle Percy leaning against a stall. Uncle Percy had gotten himself to his feet at the shot and was breathing heavily. George motioned him to silence with his finger and unhooked the Winchester.

He could see Don and Ernie down below, illuminated in their circle of electric light. Then he looked up and he saw his mother lying on the beam. He had not seen her when he swung in above Uncle Percy. He had never seen Joelene anywhere except with both feet on the ground. She was terrified of heights, everybody knew that. He held his breath as he watched her. He could see that Joelene was trying to cut the rope that held up one of the sandbags.

Joelene was having trouble getting the knife to cut all

the way through. Suddenly something happened. George couldn't be sure what happened but in a final desperate bid to cut through the rope, Joelene reached too far, she felt herself slipping and she gasped and the knife fell from her hand. Below, Don and Ernie suddenly looked up, pinpointing where she was. Ernie held up the light and Don screamed, "You bitch!" and fired his gun. The bullet whined past her and Joelene cried out and began to squirm backward along the beam. Don took aim again but George stood up at the edge of the deck, his legs firmly planted, his mouth tight, his eye fixing Don Diamond exactly in his sights.

"Drop it, Don," he shouted.

Don swung around to the voice and squeezed off another shot. It whined overhead, but George didn't move. He remembered what Uncle Percy had said—"Don't hold your breath" and "Shoot a little lower"—and he did and he felt the recoil against his shoulder and as his bullet found Don he saw him spin around and drop to the ground. Ernie screamed and let off a volley of loose shots that made George duck, and then he felt the Winchester being taken from him and Uncle Percy raised the gun and aimed it at Ernie and squeezed the trigger and Ernie fell down and grabbed his leg. Ernie let off one more shot and hit one of the suspended sandbags, which burst open and began to rain down hundred-dollar bills, and Ernie started to cry.

Somewhere in the distance—or was it just outside?—

they heard the siren of the fire engine. George looked at Uncle Percy and saw that there were snowflakes on his glasses. He looked up at the sky. It had begun to snow.

"Sit me down, George," said Uncle Percy. An eerie light had filled the ark as the snow and the sulfuric sky mingled. "Sit me down, George," said Uncle Percy again, as George tried to make him comfortable. "You tell them now, I shot them. I shot both the men."

"Uncle Percy—"

"Listen, George. You do this for me. It only complicates your life to carry something you don't need. You understand me?"

Down below a commotion had begun as the firemen and the troopers and the children and the adults streamed into the ark. Spinning green bills and snow drifted down on them. Lights flashed and sound blared, but around Uncle Percy there was a pearly silence.

"Got something for you," said Uncle Percy, trying to find his way into a pocket of his pajamas under the blanket.

"Uncle Percy, don't talk. I'll get help."

"I got all the help I need," said Uncle Percy, pressing something cold into George's hand.

George opened his fingers. "A brass handle," he said.

"For the door," said Uncle Percy. His voice had fallen to a whisper. "I never needed a way out." George sensed his mother coming up beside them. She was trembling and white but her concern was all for Uncle Percy.

"Is he coming now?" asked Uncle Percy. Joelene touched his hand while George supported him.

"Yes, Uncle Percy, he's coming."

Now I didn't see anything, and neither did anyone else I spoke to, but that didn't stop the rumors and I can't get my mother to budge from her story. She said she saw something. It was probably just one of the sandbags moving, or a reveler who had got up the stairs before anyone else did. Besides, it was dim. There was a sulfuric light. It was snowing. It was raining down dollar bills.

Dad said she'd just been looking at the fireworks and the negative imprint was still on her eyeballs. Her eyes were just playing tricks on her, but there was a weird light, everyone said so, so perhaps—oh, I don't know. Much as I long to believe that Uncle Percy's soul soared out of his ark that night, I can't.

Still, funny things have happened since that Halloween. Funny, good things. First of all there was a renewed surge of churchgoing, almost a revival, and even the *New York Times* sent up a reporter to see what was going on.

Mom was interviewed on a breakfast television show, and she was so shocked at seeing how she looked on film that she took herself off to Weight Watchers and things haven't been the same since.

No one ever claimed the money, and Uncle Sam still has it deposited somewhere safe, I suppose, or it has all been absorbed by boring things like macadam roads or upstate sewage plants. It was amazing, though, how little was actually found, as it seemed a heck of a lot drifted down that night onto little hobgoblins and their parents. A few new televisions were bought, some VCRs and stereos, some kids got sent to college, but no one got rich.

Uncle Percy left his house to Joelene, and Joelene and Pete got married the following year. Joelene planted a wisteria over the front porch. Pete buys her a packet of gummy bears every Saturday morning at the diner when they come in for a coffee. Pete still cooks.

My dad finally got to like—well, not *like,* exactly—Mike Astanazy, and when he got accepted into the police force, Dad sort of accepted the inevitable as well. So Mike and Geraldine got engaged.

Parrish hasn't changed. He never will. He looks after the ark for Joelene. The ark hasn't changed. It just sits there and we all take it for granted, like a rose bed at the back of somebody's garden that you never notice after a while.

As for George, he went back to school and worked Saturdays at the hardware store. After college, George wants to go to Hollywood and make movies. In May, I graduate from high school and George is taking me to the prom. He says my head looks a lot like Uncle Percy's, and he likes that. I still want to be a writer. George says I could make a lot of money as a scriptwriter in Hollywood. He says we could drive the Mustang there. Dad says over his dead body. Well, we'll see.